THE TERMINAL BAR

A NOVEL BY LARRY MITCHELL

For Dolores,
We did have some
fun, even tho it was
school.
Larry R. Mitchell
NYC, Nov. 1985

CALAMUS BOOKS • BOX 689 • COOPER STATION • N.Y.C. 10276

ISBN 0-930762-05-3

Library of Congress # 82-70633

Cover Photo and Book Design:	Joseph Modica
Back Cover Photos taken from the Italian Television program "Invecce della Famiglia":	Allan Mandel
Clouds and Limos:	Bill Rice
Typeset:	Foto-Ready, NYC Herb Fields Studio, NYC
Printed:	Print Center, Brooklyn, USA

First printing, April, 1982
1 2 3 4 5 6 7 8 9 10

I lifted a great deal of this novel from the lives of a small circle of my friends. I want to thank them for doing what they did in the way they did it and for allowing me to be a part of it. This book is for them.

NOTE ON SOURCES
The public events in this novel are certified by the *New York Times* to have actually happened. Some of the other events, the less public ones, also actually happened. But many of them did not. The Terminal Bar is a real place, though it goes by a different name.

CONTENTS

LIVING IN THE CENTER OF THE EMPIRE

Robin cannot remember the exact year Salvador Allende was assassinated. Annoyed, he wipes himself, pulls up his red painter pants, and flushes the toilet. Preoccupied by the image of planes bombing the Chilean presidential palace, he wanders down the long hall which slopes slightly to the left, into the kitchen.

Two cats rush at him from the adjoining living room. Auden is screaming. 'A mistake,' Robin thinks, moving out of the kitchen backwards. They surround him. "O.K., O.K. Eat yourselves into oblivion." He pours some dry food onto a plate. Gloria, large and white with a black tail, sprawls on the floor and lays his head on the plate. Auden, skinny and orange, nibbles delicately at each separate kernel.

Robin retreats into the living room and collapses into the lavender sofa and onto an old *New York Times.* He pulls it out from under him. "So what news of the empire do we have here?" he asks as he leafs swiftly through the pages. His mind goes on hold until he sees a picture of homosexual men being executed in Iran. He stares at the picture for a long time and then sighs. 'Another revolution which doesn't want us.'

He tosses the paper aside and lies down on the sofa. Auden approaches, meows and leaps onto his stomach. "Hi, pousse," he says, rubbing Auden's ears. "They are slaughtering faggots in Iran. What do you think Mama Cat should do about it?" Robin thinks for a moment. "It is either get depressed or get stoned." Auden moves up Robin's body and licks his chin. "Get stoned it is." He swings himself up. Auden leaps onto the back of the lavender sofa where he vigorously sharpens his claws, pulling out three tufts of cotton before he settles down. The cotton tufts float to the floor. Robin turns abruptly to him. "Ah—but the question remains: on what? Maybe a blend. A little of this and a little of that. That's clever, since a little is all I have of anything." He reaches for a small tin box on the round wooden table in front of him and opens it. He takes out half a Quaalude and lays it on the table. He goes to the kitchen, trips over Gloria, who is still sprawled on the bare wooden floor, recovers and gets a beer from the refrigerator. He sets it on the table and himself on the sofa and begins to roll a joint. At the moment he is about to lick the paper the phone rings. It startles him. The paper slips and the grass falls on the table. Auden leaps from the sofa to the table to investigate. Robin picks up the phone to hear a too familiar question.

"What did I do? Tell me. No, don't tell me. Was I too wicked at the bar last night? Was I beyond the beyond?" Rosa babbles into the phone, trying to defuse any anger.

"This is Rosa of the famous Rugosa family, I take it?"

"The very same."

"What do you remember?" Robin asks firmly.

"I had a wonderful time. We danced and kissed all evening."

"You don't remember stealing people's drinks and pouring them down the toilet?"

"But I wouldn't do a thing like that," Rosa protests.

Robin continues sternly. "Each time you poured another drink down the toilet you yelled 'White man's poison.' You embarrassed a lot of people." Rosa is gasping denials. "Barnaby tried to hit you and Emma left in disgust. You only stopped when a stranger, to whom you'd done this, locked you in the bathroom."

"That must be why I had all that toilet paper in my pocket this morning. Oh, it must have been amusing. Too bad I missed it."

"Others won't soon forget." It had recently become popular in Robin's circle for people to do any outrageous thing that came into their heads and then, if anyone got upset, to claim memory loss. "Rosa, it is important to remember so at least you can feel guilty. Guilt is the only thing that keeps us on this side of the line. Otherwise we'd all go over the edge."

"Which edge are you talking about exactly? I feel over some edge all the time."

"It is important to remember, otherwise you will begin to repeat your outrages and that gets very tedious very quickly."

"Oh, darling, I know. But most of my life is so much like the rest of my life that I don't need to remember it. You will just have to write my memories for me. You know so much more about me than I do. After all, there was that torrid romance of ours when I was a mere child and you an older gentleman."

"You were twenty-five and your name was Marvin," Robin sneers. The story of their romance has developed over the years into a trashy soap opera and Robin has heard it too many times. It is Rosa's favorite story, however, and he never misses an opportunity to go over it once more.

"How I loved you—totally, obsessively, passionately, blissfully—and you threw me over, breaking my heart and sending me into the gutters of despair." Rosa reaches his favorite part and raises his voice for effect. "And for what? Trash who treated you like dirt. But you loved it. You couldn't take real love from a real queen. No, you wanted pain from cheap tricks."

Their break-up had been hard. Rosa went into a year of heavy depression because he was losing what he knew he wanted. Robin cried for months because he was giving up what he had hoped he wanted but didn't. Since then they had become friends, the kind of friends who spot each other's lies the second they are told.

"But you have to admit for someone as fucked up as me, some of those tricks turned out to be pretty delicious. I notice you managed to get a few of them into your bed," Robin chuckles.

"That"—Rosa is adamant—"is another story. You always change the subject just when I start to tell you the truth. But no matter, after last night my reputation is obviously ruined."

"Rosa, it is a waste of time to regret losing something you never had."

"I must put my apology into the dish that's going around."

"That's easy. Call anyone we know. Everyone's discussing you. You were the evening's scandal. You know how excited everyone gets over a scandal."

"I can barely move my body; my head is bouncing off the wall and they expect me to show up and cheerfully drag dirty dishes around that restaurant. Those people leave enough food on their plates to feed every bum on the street—and I mean feed them"

"They pay you at least."

"It's barely subway fare." Rosa laments, "I'm thirty-five years old and still a busboy. What does it mean?"

"You're not upwardly mobile."

"I'm a diva," he announces. "We divas sit on drugstore stools and wait to be discovered. We do not have to be pushy about success."

"Just smile and look sexy. Someone is bound to notice."

"By the time I'm discovered I'll only be fit to play burnt-out beauticians or retired librarians. But what else can I do except look for love and hope for fame? Oh, hon, I've got to go put on my work drag and fly off. I'm too late already. Soon." The phone goes dead as Robin notices that his half Quaalude is no longer on the table and neither is Auden. He leaps up, runs around the apartment yelling at Auden, who is in hiding.

He returns to the sofa and lifts it up. He finds five wine bottle corks, hidden there by Gloria, three pornographic magazines and a dead mouse, but no pill. 'They're killing homosexuals in Iran and I can't get off in New York. It's the center of the empire and I can't get stoned.' He kicks the dead mouse into the center of the room and picks up the magazines. Gloria slides down the side of a chair, walks cautiously up to the dried carcass, sniffs and turns his back on it. Robin sits on the sofa and thumbs through one of the magazines. Dust flies out of it, forming a small cloud. Robin sneezes three times while batting at the dust. In self-defense he pushes the three magazines back under the sofa. Noting the grass on the table, he carefully cleans it up and is about to roll a joint when the phone rings again.

"It's Emma here. I thought you would want to know at once that I have quit my therapy group."

"Oh?" says Robin, knowing the worst is yet to come.

"I don't feel real anymore. My life does not seem real. And I see no point in trying to get integrated and healthy when I am not real—and I told them all so tonight."

Realizing it is nothing serious, Robin relaxes. "Maybe it's the drugs," he suggests. "You may have become permanently stoned."

"Scarlet thinks it's all the poisons around. She says our brains are mutating as our bodies collapse. But I don't know. I even masturbated twice today and I still don't feel real."

Robin puts the phone between his ear and his shoulder and rolls his joint. "When was the last time you felt real?"

"It's hard to remember. When we used to do acid. That was real."

"It was too real for me."

"Why did we stop doing acid? I can't remember."

"Because it became impossible to say 'far out' when we saw so clearly that the planet was being slowly destroyed and, as an afterthought, us with it. I remember one summer day riding on a Greyhound bus through New Jersey. An old woman was sitting next to me. She poked me in the side and pointed out the window at an orange opaque sky and an open sewer that once might have been a river. In a sad voice she said, 'The earth can't take much more of that kinda treatment. How can a person live without the air or the water?' After that I went right for the Quaaludes and the Jack Daniels."

Emma laughs self-mockingly. "When terrified go numb. It is how we've gotten through it all, isn't it?"

"This place is too scary to have an expanded consciousness in. No wonder you don't feel real." Robin hears Emma take a loud drink of something. He sips his beer and lights his joint.

They had met ten years before at a sit-in in the dean's office at Queens College. Emma was straight then and got an immediate crush on Robin. When she found out he was gay, and realized that the last five men she had had crushes on were all gay, she began to wonder what was going on. But since she always thought lesbians were glamorous and rich and lived in Paris and she was only glamorous, she figured she couldn't be a lesbian. Then the women's liberation movement came along. She hates to miss anything, so when all her women friends started saying we've got to love each other and then began to do precisely that, Emma could not resist.

"Well, you've cheered me right up. Who wants to feel real in a place like this anyway? I may be the healthiest person in my group."

"Are you still quitting?"

"I think so. At the rate I'm going, by the time I'm well adjusted there won't be anything left to be adjusted to. How can you adjust to nuclear annihilation and chemical poisoning anyway? I might as well turn on the TV and let it turn my mind into mashed potatoes."

"You're so in touch with the culture."

"The only thing I'm in touch with these days is what's between my legs. I guess I'll go masturbate during the Mary Tyler Moore rerun," she says cheerfully. She sends kiss sounds into the phone and hangs up.

Robin remembers a survey he did on his friends about their frequency of masturbation. Emma won easily since one, two, or even three orgasms only made her hornier. It was only after the fourth or fifth one that she began to be able to think of doing something else. 'Amazing capacity,' he thinks as he goes to the refrigerator for another can of beer. He puts an old Aretha Franklin album on and dances around the room feeling slightly horny. Gloria becomes alarmed and hides.

Feeling dizzy, he sits down. When his head stops spinning, he is thinking about brawny, mean-faced generals issuing orders to low-flying planes spraying Agent Orange over dying Vietnamese jungles and pilots dropping bombs from B-52's on the people of Hanoi on Christmas Day. Realizing this way of thinking will only make him depressed, he drinks some beer and gets up to turn the Aretha record over.

'I could go the bar,' he thinks, 'but what time is it?' He rushes into the kitchen and looks at a small electric clock with half its plastic casing missing. It says 9:00. 'Can that be right?' He watches the clock to see if it is running. The second hand jerks erratically around the dial as a cockroach walks lazily over the numbers. 'If I go to the bar now, by the time anybody gets there I'll be too drunk to talk. But if I stay home, I'll just sit around and think about the generals and get depressed.' Having created for himself a clear choice, he moves around the apartment turning off lights and admonishing the cats to be good. He notices the mouse carcass, picks it up by its scrawny tail and drops it in the garbage. Gloria watches indifferently. He grabs his puffy down coat, flings a crocheted scarf around his neck and walks down the long, slanted hall toward the door. His shoe crunches on something. He looks down and sighs. He wets his finger and picks up a smashed half Quaalude. He tries to separate the dirt from the flakes of pill but fails. He licks his finger and makes a face. 'You gotta eat dirt to get stoned around here,' he thinks, sauntering out the door to the Terminal Bar.

2

THERE'S ALWAYS LIFE AT THE TERMINAL BAR

Arriving in front of the piece of plywood that serves as the door to the Terminal Bar, Robin notices he has stepped in dog shit. He wipes the dog shit off his shoe, opens the door, and walks out of the cold, damp air into the chilly, smoky bar. Women surround the pool table on the left and men lounge along the bar on the right.

Robin and his friends consider the Terminal Bar to be their bar. The windows are covered with grime; the plants all died years ago but their dead remains continue to hang in plastic pots; the pinball machines, except for one ancient one, are all broken; the wooden floor is covered with cigarette butts and the bartenders are either surly or sweet and drunk. The owner, an old man from New Jersey, wanted it to be a busy men's cruise bar, so he hung some old chains from the ceiling, nailed a few rusty hubcaps on the walls and made the bartenders wear cowboy hats and leave their shirts unbuttoned to their navels. The bartenders are, as a result, always chilly.

Rosa discovered the bar. He called Robin at once to tell him about it. It sounded awfully down and out. Robin loved it.

"Does anyone cruise there?" he asked Rosa.

"Only a couple of hot dykes. Everyone else is too busy giving attitude or getting stoned to bother." Robin squealed with delight. "Sometimes I hear you can get a blow job in the toilet. But it has to be quick since there is only one."

The first time Robin went there, someone turned him on to coke in the toilet, his favorite place to do coke. He became a fan for life.

Robin peers through the orange, smoky light that covers

the room until he notices Barnaby at the end of the bar where the serious drinkers hang out. Barnaby is tall and angular. He is dressed, as always, in black. Robin walks the length of the bar, nodding to several half-remembered acquaintances. He and Barnaby kiss, 'with a hint of passion,' Robin thinks hopefully.

"I thought you'd be home getting ready for your party."

"It is not a party. It's an art piece. I keep telling you," Barnaby says sternly. He is sober and feeling edgy.

"I'm sorry. I forgot."

Trying for a little warmth, Barnaby asks, "What have you been doing?"

"I tried to get stoned, but Auden stole my last half Quaalude. Then I sat and thought about the Pentagon."

"That sounds depressing."

"It drove me here."

"And the half Quaalude?"

"I found it. Crushed under my shoe."

"And the Pentagon?"

"I remember hearing that when they got Kennedy, it was in reality a quiet military coup. The military did it and took over the show. They kept the outer forms the same, but they let it be known who had control of the bombs. It makes sense. Whatever the military wants, it gets—no matter how expensive or how outrageous. The fascists snuck in quietly." Robin is warming up to his subject and his persona as a radical intellectual when Barnaby gives out a loud sneer.

"They have always been in control, in one guise or another. Patriarchy and fascism are the same thing and work the same way. It doesn't matter what the men call themselves—generals, prime ministers, presidents, judges—it's always the same."

"That's rather extreme," Robin says weakly, wanting to be more moderate, even judicious, if only not to succumb to despair. "A two-thousand-year-old enemy makes me want to puke and give up." Since male culture nearly drove him crazy, he is now obsessed with it. Not with how it works—that he knows so well it is part of the natural background—but why it goes on. "I can't understand why the men keep doing competition and domination over and over again." Robin's voice begins to get full. "Most of them lose at it. Most end up both dominated and beaten in the competition. Yet on they go with it. No one is happy from what I can tell. It doesn't make anyone relaxed or friendly or content. It's a mystery to me. And for two thousand years. Amazing. But they do change their tactics now and then."

"They are always as vicious as they need to be." Barnaby stares at Robin harshly.

"They are invincible then?" Robin feels he is heading for a bummer.

"Maybe."

"Do you know how to defeat them?"

Barnaby knows he is caught now and relaxes a little. "A new religion. A new science. Or a general strike. Maybe just living our subversive lives will change it."

"Like our constant public homo sex." Robin responds to the irony in Barnaby's voice.

"More like our revolutionary disco dancing."

They both smile for the first time.

Robin and Barnaby first fell in love with each other's minds. They were both obsessed with the patriarchy. Then they got turned on to each other's bodies. However, at the time, each one was having an affair with a best friend of the other, so it was too complicated to do anything except talk and sneak an occasional feel. Unfulfilled, their passion and fantasies grew. When it finally became safe to fuck, after both their affairs were over, the reality was a slight letdown. They settled easily into a passionate friendship with occasional sex.

Robin takes a joint that is moving past him down the bar, smokes and passes it on to Barnaby.

The bartender leans over the bar. "Put the dope away quick," he says softly. "An undercover cop just walked in. We think he might be a narc." Barnaby swallows the joint.

·

"This is 1979."

"This is New York."

"Nevertheless, cool it."

"What about touching? Can they still get us for that?"

"I guess they can. But I hear they are after dope."

Barnaby leans over and kisses Robin's cheek. "If he can't take a joke, fuck him," he says, grinning.

"Which one is he?"

"The one over there. Behind you, near the pinball machine."

Barnaby turns and looks at the man. "He's not even cute."

"He's probably straight."

"A het," Robin mutters, turning slowly to get a quick peek to store in his mental file. "He is wearing polyester," he exclaims.

"Looks that way," the bartender laughs. "There's another one who's been in here too. Just as obvious."

"How do you know they're undercover?"

"Word's out on the street."

"He's a joke." Robin feels relieved.

"If he busts you, he ain't no joke," the bartender reminds Robin.

"We're cool. Just a couple of depressed fags waiting quietly for the end."

Barnaby likes Robin's description of them and leans over and gives him another kiss on the cheek.

"Cut the illegal stuff." Robin moves to slap Barnaby's cheek but the gesture changes into a caress.

Barnaby stares at Robin, wanting suddenly to lean him over the bar and fuck him. "No sex and no drugs. This could drive a person crazy."

"Could make you mean, vicious and a cop hater."

"You can't ride the subways without having your purse snatched, and they have this guy hanging out in a sleazy bar where everybody is too poor to have more than a couple of joints on them at a time."

"Shakes your faith in the rationality of the powerful."

Barnaby grabs Robin's arm. "I think he's armed. There's a bulge in his chest." He leans over and asks the bartender.

"They're always armed."

Robin closes his eyes and takes a deep breath. "There is a hired, armed killer in our bar." Robin moves quickly to the other side of Barnaby so he faces the cop. "I don't want to have my back to him. They love to shoot people in the back." Robin stares at the cop, who is shifting uncomfortably from one foot to the other. "I had a cop in a class I was teaching, once. I was talking about how rotten the system is and how we must destroy it and he lets his coat fall open so we could all see his gun. I finally told him to leave the gun at home or don't come back to class."

"What did he do?"

"He never came back." Robin sighs again and orders a double scotch. "Maybe I should try butch lessons again."

Barnaby laughs. "Did you take them once?"

"Yeah. It was a joke. I did it when butch first showed its craggy face on Christopher Street. I figured I'd never get laid again if I couldn't learn the butch stride and imitate the somber look. Sometimes I could actually keep my wrist straight, my chest raised, my ass tight, my brow furrowed and my mouth shut. But then I'd have a couple drinks and before I'd know it, I'd be as fey as ever. I was hopeless. And as Christopher Street got butcher, I got more militantly swish. I even got to love my small pot belly. I decided it was a Buddha belly. Round bellies are spiritual, flat stomachs are military." He pauses. "However, my butch lessons were abandoned forever when I realized it did not affect how often I got laid. It wasn't all that much either way."

"And you want to go through that again?"

"There is an armed killer in this bar. What do you suggest? I don't think it's that cool to stand out as much as I do when these men have blood on their minds, not to mention their hands."

13

Barnaby strokes Robin's cheek and smiles at him.

"Do you feel obviously queer?"

"I forget how obvious I am until I am walking down the street and the sun is shining and people are actually smiling and someone calls me a faggot. Then I remember."

"At the coding office, nearly everyone is queer, but no one talks about it. I hate that. Some dirty little secret we all have. It makes me get provocative. I talked today about cocksucking in a very loud voice. It was very tacky." Barnaby is snorting with pleasure. He laughs through his nose.

"Did you talk about a cock you had sucked?"

"No, one I saw someone else suck. Well, actually not one. He sucked eleven while I watched." Robin coos in appreciation. "It was in a public tearoom below Houston Street. All black and Hispanic men. Some watched the door, some masturbated, and some sat on the toilets and sucked any cock that was put in their mouths."

"Fags aren't usually so democratic."

"White fags, you mean."

"What did you do there?"

"I watched. It was hot. But, for some reason, I don't want to have sex with anybody these days."

Robin is alarmed. "How long has this been going on?" He tries to remember the last time they slept together, but can't.

"At least a couple of weeks now."

"Let's hope it passes."

"It had better pass and soon. Since I firmly believe that all violence comes from sexual repression, I wonder what the fuck I am doing to myself."

"Getting ready for war, no doubt."

"All clear. You can live it up again," the bartender announces. Chatting, they had not noticed the narc leave.

"Great. I ate my last joint," Barnaby grumbles and orders a whisky sour.

"Look who is coming through the door," Robin says, nodding towards a short, skinny man with a shaved head and a

14

short, tattered jacket.

"What is he doing here?" Barnaby asks, looking revolted.

"I thought you two were friends."

"We were. But he's too sneaky for me. Besides, he's straight."

"Maybe he is here to change his orientation."

"Oh, no, not that. He is a repulsive person. We already have J. Edgar Hoover. That's plenty to live down. Between him and J. Edgar, fags could get a bad name." Barnaby is agitated. "Don't look at him, he might catch it."

"I used to think that it was impossible to be a faggot and a fascist at the same time. Old J. Edgar sure blew that idea to shit." Robin's mind drifts to the FBI. "Hoover was clever, though, you have to give him that. He took the classic tactic hets use against us. You know the one—get the dirt on us and then blackmail us with it. He took that and used it against every powerful straight man in the country. His files sizzled. And when he wanted something, they got it for him." Robin pauses and sips his drink.

"That's the price they pay for hypocrisy," Barnaby observes. "No one could ever blackmail us since all our dirty laundry is already hanging out in public." Barnaby finishes his whisky sour suddenly. "I'm leaving. A cop and a het in the bar in one evening. It's enough to drive me to a disco." He takes hold of Robin's face with both his hands and gives him a wet kiss on the mouth. "See you tomorrow," he says, grabbing his coat and striding to the door.

Barnaby's abrupt exit leaves Robin confused. "I'm alone. Fuck." He orders another double scotch, not noticing that his last one is half full. A joint floats by him. He takes a long puff and passes it without noticing the person he passes it to.

"Aren't you going to say hello?"

Robin opens his eyes and focuses on Charlie. He remembers that they live together and announces, "You should not be surprised tonight when you get home if you notice that I am not speaking to Auden."

"He pissed on your pillow again."

"He stole my last half Quaalude," Robin states. Remembering what Charlie's life is like these days, he asks, "Why aren't you at the theater? It's still early."

"The play ended quite early tonight. They dropped so many lines, it only lasted an hour. They left out at least half the second act, which left the three people in the audience quite confused."

"Three people?"

"Yeah, I figured I'd better put up some posters." He holds up a bucket with evaporated milk and a brush in it.

"Let me see one." Charlie puts a poster on the bar. It is a picture of two men dressed in grass skirts embracing. The title, "Too Much Heat in the Amazon," streaks across the top in red letters. Robin squints. The bar's orange light makes it look faded. "Where is your name?"

Charlie points to "Stage Manager: Charlie Dove" at the bottom. "Knowing you'd be here, I thought I'd stop by and have a quick drink." He orders a shot of scotch.

Robin notices a hint of disapproval in Charlie's voice and knows it's because Charlie has found him at the bar so early. Not to be outdone, he says sarcastically, "It's nice to see you, for a change." He is about to launch into his current complaint about how he never sees Charlie anymore when he notices his two drinks. Embarrassed, he gulps down the half-full one, choking on it. Charlie slaps him on the back. Robin sputters, "There was an armed killer in here tonight..."

"You mean a cop?" Charlie asks hopefully.

"A narc."

"What did he do?"

"He kept us from smoking a joint and from making out for over an hour." A grin spreads over Charlie's face. Robin shows a slight smile and protests, "It is scary when they're armed."

"I know," Charlie says soothingly. "But no one was hurt or arrested. Right?"

Robin shakes his head no, staring gloomily into an orange light bulb in a wall fixture.

Charlie puts his nose on Robin's cheek and nuzzles it. "Do you want me to stay here with you?"

Robin is surprised. "Of course not. I'm fine."

Charlie nuzzles him again. "I'll see you at home later." He downs his shot, picks up his pail and his posters and leaves.

'If I only knew what to call him,' Robin thinks, 'then I could be more relaxed. We do share a bed and an apartment. But we hardly ever have sex. So we can't be lovers. But it's more than just having a roommate. Maybe we are boyfriends.' He gulps down half of his full drink. 'There is no point in trying to figure it out; it doesn't matter what I call our relationship. It is what it is. I'm too hung up on words and concepts.'

He looks around glumly and orders another drink.

3

APPROACHING NUMBNESS

Robin cannot decide what to wear. He stares blankly at his few clothes hanging from hooks on the bedroom wall. "Too tired. I must do something about my wardrobe," he says to Gloria, who is sitting near him also staring blankly at his clothes. Not having many clothes makes it easier to decide what to wear each morning and easier to pack. Easy packing is essential, he figures, if he should ever have to escape quickly. So far he has not been forced into hiding, but his knowledge of pogroms, deportations, roundups and quick and brutal crackdowns on the left is too vast for him to be complacent. "Half what I do is illegal, and the other half is disapproved of, so I must be prepared," he once told his mother. He takes a pair of blue jeans from a hook and puts them on.

He walks down the long hall to a large closet. It is filled with clothes left by people who have passed through his apartment. He always urges visitors to take whatever they need. But people always leave more than they take. In the closet, he finds Auden asleep in a shopping bag, a pousse print blouse, and a long black scarf. With his cigarette, he burns a hole in the blouse where he thinks his nipple will be. He slips the blouse on. The hole is too high. It only reveals a mole. 'But it is a hole, and holes are in,' he thinks. He wraps the scarf around his neck and pins it together with an enameled pink triangle.

He walks to the bathroom to examine the effect. 'I look ridiculous.' He puts some kohl on his eyes and a touch of rouge on his lips. Just a touch. Always in moderation. Even as a hippie, he never wore more than one necklace at a time.

He is ready. 'Early as usual,' he thinks, 'so eager to party. A sure sign of a frivolous nature.' He sits down on the lavender sofa, stuffing some cotton back under the upholstery, next to Gloria, who is lying on his back, exposing a large white stomach. Gloria opens his eyes and stretches his legs into the air, signaling that a pet is due. Robin ignores the hint so Gloria rolls over, sits up, walks into his lap and meows. Robin smiles and rubs his head and then his back as Gloria turns around three times in his lap and then collapses. "Gloria, I think that you have arranged this entire household for your own benefit and pleasure. How smart you must be."

The phone rings. Robin sits up straight and Gloria springs to the floor, issuing a loud complaint.

"Hi, hon." It is Charlie. "I have to put up posters again, so I'll be late for the party. Why don't you go on and I'll meet you there."

"Are you really coming?"

"Oh, I don't know. I'm tired. Maybe I'll just come home and putter around there." Charlie's greatest pleasure is to get stoned and rearrange the furniture.

"Well, whatever."

"See you later." Charlie makes three smacking sounds into the phone and hangs up.

The phone rings again.

"Are you ready for this?" Rosa yells breathlessly.

"Well, I'm dressed, if that's what you mean."

"Are you taking drugs?"

"I'll take a Quaalude in my stomach if you'll bring me one and some joints in my pocket."

"I'll bring, I'll bring. Try not to get too nervous. What I need is some coke. I'm exhausted."

"Too much sex?"

"Too much work. I just finished painting my apartment. Very New York. All white. Too white. Too bright. Oh, I hope I behave tonight. There's the buzzer. Must be Emma. We'll be over soon."

Robin hangs up and sighs. 'I'll never stay sober tonight,' he thinks. Auden screams in the kitchen, demanding food. Robin

20

walks into the kitchen, takes a can and opens it. Auden jumps on the table, then off the table and then back on it again. Gloria rouses himself from the floor and saunters in for supper. Putting the dish of food on the floor, Robin trips over Auden and kicks their water dish. Mopping up, cursing, he notices the avocado plant drooping badly. He waters it, which leads to watering the two spider plants, the four ferns, the one begonia, the three wandering jews, the four violets and the one orange tree. Walking around watering the plants, he notices that all the ashtrays are full, a week's worth of the *New York Times* is scattered about and the towels in the bathroom smell of mildew. Though Robin hates to clean, he loves to straighten up, especially if he can make the place look neat in less than five minutes.

After this frantic excursion he collapses into a chair to smoke a cigarette and continue his newest fantasy—the trial of Henry Kissinger. The fantasy has recently bogged down over a couple of difficulties. For one, he cannot figure out how to capture Kissinger. 'We'll have to follow him around for a while, study his habits carefully, pick a moment and snatch him off the street. Once we've got him, we'll drive him to a rented house in Allentown, Pennsylvania. We'll seal off the basement and stash him there. We'll let him have a cot to sleep on and a bottle to piss in. He can eat off the floor with his hands, nothing but overcooked vegetables. That will unnerve him. He'll feel like his strength is failing him. I'll sit with him every day and let him reminisce. I'll tape it all. As the weeks pass and no one rescues him, he will panic. We'll hold a trial in this damp, dark basement. He will be found guilty of excessive war crimes and sentenced to death. He'll be unhinged with fear. We'll make a deal. We'll reduce his sentence if he names names. Who killed Kennedy; who ordered Allende overthrown; who knew about the secret bombing of Cambodia; who, in the CIA, teaches torture techniques. We'll then turn all this information over to the *New York Times*, who will, no doubt, refuse to publish it. This is my other small problem. They certainly won't publish the stuff to save K's life, not after he has squealed on all his famous friends. Maybe the *New York Review of Books* will pick it up, or the *Village Voice*. It will be so juicy, someone will publish it. Once we've dragged every last secret out of him, we'll dump him, drugged, on a quiet street in Queens, a broken man, a pariah among his rich fascist friends.' He sighs with pleasure. 'What a delicious fantasy. One of my best in weeks.' His mind drifts back to the interrogation in the basement. 'What other crimes can I ask him about?'

The phone rings. "Shit. Hello."

"This is Maybellene Donit," sounding distraught.

"What's wrong, hon?"

"I have nothing to wear. I've had on every outfit I own and they all look like shit. Marie just called and yelled at me—yelled at me!—for ignoring her at the dyke dance last night, which I didn't do. I didn't even see her. I don't even remember the dance. And Susan B. just threw up her dinner and now wants more food."

"Well," thinking quickly of some way to be useful, "come over and look through the big closet. And bring Susan B. along. She can fight with Auden. It'll take her mind off her problems."

"Oh, maybe I shouldn't go. Emma is going, I take it."

"Yeah."

"Is she still mad at me?"

"Well, she isn't mad exactly. She just thought it a bit rude to go on and on about how small her breasts were compared to yours."

"Oh, I thought she was upset because I was feeling her up in the bar."

"I think it's O.K. now."

"I'm not responsible these days."

"None of us are. Now come over."

The moment he hangs up, the phone rings.

"Oh, sweets, this is Barnaby. Can you bring those tapes I left there when you come? You are coming, aren't you?"

"Of course, I'm just waiting for the maniacs to pick me up.

What tapes?"

"The ones I played for you."

"Of police sirens and breaking glass and dial tones?"

"Yeah."

"But this is a party."

"I keep telling you it is an art piece posing as a party. They will give just the right mood to the place. I've covered the walls with huge pictures...oh, you'll see. Bring them?"

"O.K. What are you on?" knowing this is an appropriate question to ask Barnaby at any time of day or night.

"Oh, just a little opium. Nothing else, yet."

"There's my buzzer. Soon." He kisses the telephone receiver, getting saliva on it, and hangs up.

Maybellene sweeps through the door. Susan B. leaps out of her arms and runs down the hall in hot pursuit of the cats' food dish. Gloria, not wanting to be hassled, waddles into the closet while Auden hisses and tries to be butch. Susan B. hisses back. They both sit down, staring at each other, for a good hiss.

"Maybe they'll fall in love. Have an affair. We could certainly use a hot romance around here. Romance has been in very short supply lately," she says as she walks into the closet in search of the perfect outfit. Robin retreats to the sofa.

"Our bag lady's back," Maybellene yells from the closet.

"How's she doing?"

"Great. She's teaching herself Spanish. Figures if she's going to work in this neighborhood, she'd better learn the language."

"Did she say where she's been all winter?"

"Just uptown visiting friends."

"Other bag ladies?"

"She didn't say. She's very secretive. She said someone bought her a pack of cigarettes but she didn't like the brand so she traded them with a junior high school boy for his Spanish book."

Maybellene steps out of the closet dressed in a brown leather mini-skirt, black stockings and a black halter. Her white hair is standing on end. Her eyes and lips are black. "It's the best I can do with that trash in there."

The buzzer rings and the cats leap at each other, screeching. Robin steps around the cat fight. At the door, he greets Emma and Rosa with a peck on each of their cheeks. Maybellene, trying to distract the cats, lies down on the kitchen floor near the food dishes and pretends to eat Auden's food. Auden notices, turns around, walks to his kitty litter box and takes a smelly shit. Everyone screams, "How rude!" and rushes for the purer air of the living room.

Robin says to Emma, "Your breasts look full and succulent tonight."

"I had to pad them to keep my critics at bay." Maybellene's hand goes for one of them. Emma slaps it away.

Rosa throws a look of death at Robin and begins to babble. "I have made a decision."

"That's impossible," Emma declares.

"It was you who inspired me, Emma. If you can live without therapy, I can live without romance. I am not falling in love anymore."

"Don't be foolish," Robin scoffs. "What else is there to do?"

"I just don't believe in it anymore."

Maybellene, wishing to stop such nonsense before it spreads, cries, "Then you'll have to stop being a faggot."

"Never!"

"You can't be a faggot if you don't believe in romance."

"When I don't even know if there will be a tomorrow, I find it impossible to have the necessary faith to pursue romance."

"Oh, it's a religious crisis."

"You ex-Catholics always have problems with faith."

"I ask myself, what causes the most pain and frustration in my life? The answer is obvious. This absurd belief that romance will find me and rescue me from the pits of gloom." He is so earnest that they begin to think he might be serious. "Besides,

24

romance distracts you from the revolution."

"What revolution, may I ask? Am I missing something?" Maybellene's voice reeks with sarcasm.

Emma perks up. "There was something to believe in—the revolution. And I must admit I could believe in it again in a minute with the slightest encouragement."

Maybellene leans near to Emma, sneering, "Except by the time we'd win there would be nothing left to enjoy. Victorious on a dead planet. You are now the proud owner of the wasteland. Rosa, you'd better hang on to romance. I don't see much else left to believe in these days."

"I will not allow my life to be governed by a tingle in my groin, a flutter in my stomach and an unsteady heartbeat. It is time to give the old death vibe to romance. From now on this beauty is off duty." He is on his feet, bobbing up and down.

Emma looks at him pityingly. "Oh, honey, when you fall it is going to be all the way down."

"Down, down," they are all on their feet singing, "Down, down, get down."

"Don't worry," Robin says reassuringly, "if you do fall for someone, you probably won't remember it anyway. Just keep your memory loss and you'll survive. Now let's all take our pills. Here's some warm beer to wash them down with."

After several admonitions to the cats, they leave the apartment slightly wobbly. The evening is cold and damp. A fine black powder is falling out of the sky.

"We should have brought our umbrellas."

"Don't breathe until we get there."

They walk down Second Avenue towards Houston. Maybellene waves to an old woman across the street. She is huddled in a doorway, surrounded by plastic shopping bags and covered with small pieces of different-colored cloth. She raises her head from her book, sticks out her tongue, and then resumes her reading.

"I guess we're not that close anymore."

Drunks leaning against buildings, lying in doorways, and

sprawling on the sidewalk ask them for money and cigarettes. They stop at a bodega to buy more cigarettes. At Houston Street, a huge metal drum is burning. A group of ragged men stand around it keeping warm and passing a bottle. The wind catches a burning newspaper, rips it out of the drum and sends it hurling at them. They scream and scatter. The men laugh at them good-naturedly.

They regroup on the other side of Houston and enter an area abandoned first by landlords, then by the city and, finally, by the tenants. Barnaby's building stands alone on an empty block. Everything is rubble around it.

"It's like Berlin after the war down here," Emma says, trying to hide her nervousness. They suddenly freeze as two large rats dash out of the piles of bricks and rotting garbage and flee to a burnt-out building on the other side of the street.

"The nerve," Rosa shrieks in horror.

"Brazen little fuckers, aren't they?"

They walk as quickly as they can to Barnaby's building. The front door is open. A man is passed out in the hallway, his face in a pool of puke. They step over him and start up the stairs. Only Barnaby and two other tenants remain in the building, everyone else having fled to some other slum long ago. Walking up the dirty, shaky stairway, they finally hear a piercing buzz and relax, knowing they will soon be safe at Barnaby's.

4

AN ART PIECE POSING AS A PARTY

"Did you bring the tapes?" Barnaby asks slyly out of the corner of his mouth. His black hair is pasted flat on his head and shines. He is wearing a black T-shirt and black, shiny pants, 'something synthetic no doubt,' Robin thinks. He has a faraway glint in his eye, 'probably the opium,' Robin speculates.

Barnaby has transformed his apartment. The walls and the floor are bright white. Harsh white spotlights make it nearly painful to look around. Covering the walls are enormous photos of South African blacks being shot and beaten by white policemen. He took the pictures originally from his television set, then enlarged them and enlarged them until the images began to bleed into the background. The sound of sobbing is coming from one speaker and Nina Simone from the other. There is a slight rotting odor.

A few people are already there, most of whom Robin knows only by sight, members, he notices, of the radical avant garde or "the avant" as they call it.

Robin and his friends are reluctant to take off their coats. They feel they should be prepared to leave at any moment. They wander through the three small rooms. Suddenly a siren blares from a speaker. They huddle together in a corner feeling assaulted and vulnerable.

"Throw your coats in the closet," Barnaby advises as he glides by, his black patent leather shoes never leaving the floor. They obey like children faced with superior authority.

Staring at a picture of terrified black children being gunned down by white policemen, Emma says haltingly, "These pictures are eerie. They make me feel guilty being here having a good time."

"Are you having a good time?" Robin asks.

"Well, no, not really. I just got a headache and my stomach is queasy. Actually I feel rotten."

"So it's perfect. The right place to feel miserable and guilty. Is Scarlet coming here?"

"No. She's at home waiting for her period to arrive. If it comes she'll be over."

"I need a drink," Robin says as Rosa moves beside him.

"Did you see the bathtub yet?" Rosa asks, looking a trifle faint.

"Not recently."

"There are dead fish floating in it."

"Probably drank the tap water."

"That's where the liquor is. I couldn't stay to make a drink."

Not thinking, Robin says, "I'll go and get you something. Wine O.K.?"

The bathtub is full of brownish water and three large white fish float on their sides in it. The smell has saturated the room. Robin grabs a bottle of cheap white wine, two paper cups, and flees to the kitchen. A woman he does not know is throwing up in the sink. He watches her. A queasy feeling runs through his body. He flees into the next room, running into Emma and Barnaby.

"Those fish stink," Emma is exclaiming.

"They're supposed to." Barnaby is being patient. "That's what happens when something dies. It stinks."

"I feel sick. I need to sit down."

"Lie there on the floor and act wounded. You'll match the pictures."

Emma drops onto the floor. Her dramatic flair immediately catches hold of her and she begins moaning and twisting and grimacing. Bruce begins taking pictures of her, doing his fashion photographer routine.

"I read that white South African farmers are buying up land in Bolivia. They will move there when the race war gets too hot for them," Robin announces to Barnaby, trying to find something appropriate to say. "I guess they figure the Indians will be easy to keep under control." Emma gags and groans and twitches on the floor.

"Then they can visit with their German Nazi friends who all moved to Paraguay after the war."

"So that's where they went."

"They all got good jobs training the police force and setting up concentration camps for the Indians. Nazis only feel secure if they have some group to exterminate."

"The exporting of European culture has been such a charming business."

Suddenly the sound of broken glass crunches from the speakers. Rosa moves up to Robin, takes his drink and grabs his arm, pulling him away from Barnaby. "How long do we have to stay here?"

"I think until we are too numb to care anymore."

"This is a numbness party?"

"It's an art piece."

"Oh, *pardonnez-moi, mon cher.* I forgot." Rosa thinks it's all too pretentious. "Why doesn't he have pictures of faggots being beaten or American blacks being shot, or women being raped? There is enough brutality here. Why does he have to import it?"

"Maybe he didn't have his camera pointed at the TV screen when we were getting it."

"Maybe I'll take another half of a pill. That should get me to total numbness. Then I can leave."

"Then it won't matter, so you can stay."

The door flies open revealing a large number of screaming friends. The small apartment fills up. The sobbing comes back on the speakers and the smell of dead fish floats over everyone.

"I had to open the windows. Marion threw up in the sink."

"I know. I saw her do it. It's very intense, Barnaby."

"It's good for you," he says defiantly as he stalks off to change the tapes.

Emma continues writhing on the floor, forcing all the new

arrivals to step over her. Rosa leans against the wall, his eyes closed and his chest heaving. Robin cannot see Maybellene anywhere. He stands, wobbling, wondering where he might be comfortable when he feels two fingers trying to find his asshole through his pants. Ruby encircles him from behind and begins to pant in his ear. "Fuck me, it's my birthday."

"How about doing it in the bathtub?"

"I prefer the toilet bowl."

"Your place rather than mine, I take it."

Ruby is wearing tight-fitting red corduroy pants and a pink shirt open halfway down to his waist to show off his much-worked-on pecs. His hair is long, thick, black and curly. His face has classic high cheekbones and a mischievous smile. The flirt, the tease, the seducer of men and women. He is even good in bed occasionally. When he and Robin were lovers, several years ago, Robin had been threatened by Ruby's constant need to prove how attractive he was. If Ruby goes anywhere and is not propositioned at least once, he considers the outing a failure.

"How's my favorite faggot?" Ruby rubs Robin's not very well developed pecs and licks the back of his neck. Robin suddenly relaxes. He hasn't realized how hungry he is for some affectionate touching. He and Charlie seem to have a moratorium on touching as well as on sex these days. They are verbally affectionate but cut off from each other's bodies. Robin gets a hard-on. Ruby reaches down and starts rubbing Robin's hard cock.

"I can still get you hot, huh, lover boy?"

"I was fantasizing about Marlon Brando."

"And here he is. Your ass is twitching."

"Too bad your cock never gets hard enough to get in there."

"Fuck you."

"That is what I'm talking about."

Ruby swings him around and kisses him, forcing his tongue deep into Robin's mouth. Ruby is his most affectionate in public. It is his way of showing how popular he is and of proving how gay he is. He has always had difficulty convincing other people that he is a faggot. But that's because he isn't. He is bisexual, a difficult thing to be in a circle which denies that any such state exists.

Ruby is obsessed with male madness, as he calls macho. He thinks it is a disease and he knows he suffers from it. His automatic response is to hit first and ask questions later like some crazed Pentagon general. He gets sexual energy from a dirty fight like boys in a teenage gang who only fight when the odds are on their side.

When he met Robin he saw, for the first time, a man who seemed not to have been infected with macho. It intrigued him. The first time they met, Robin mistook him for a faggot and began to insult straight men. "They are hopeless. We faggots have got to stop them before they destroy us all," he had said. Ruby felt obliged to inform him that he was a straight man. Robin was horrified, immediately excused himself and headed for the bathroom. Ruby had never heard anyone denounce straight men before. He thought he might be in love. Robin was effeminate, so Ruby figured no one else would love him. 'Maybe I'll love him. He's almost like a woman. This might be fun,' he thought. So he fell in love with Robin and Robin fell in love right back. And then Robin tried to turn Ruby into a faggot. But it proved hopeless.

Robin kisses him back, then breaks away. He feels a little dizzy and knows it is because he is horny. Ruby spins out of Robin's arms to embrace Emma, who has just gotten up off the floor after someone stepped on her leg. She is stoned enough so that her aches and her guilt are tucked out of sight.

Robin moves towards the open windows in the living room. Cool winter air is blowing in to counteract the dead fish smell. He suddenly feels melancholy, an emotion he cherishes for its bittersweetness and its uselessness. His life feels overripe, full of people, love, plans, projects, work and getting high. But there is something missing, some sense of high purpose, of adventure for a grand cause outside himself. 'At least I am a faggot,' he thinks. 'That, at least, makes each day a plunge into a world not yet made. It makes all of my actions, however routine or minor, a strike against oppression.' He is a survivor. He has outwitted the self-hatred that nearly destroyed him. Now the self-loathing is specific, contained. It only appears when he does something thoughtless or when he is too selfish or too cowardly. The rest of the time he feels pleased with what he has been able to construct for himself. His life feels self-made. No one had ever taught him how to be a faggot or how to be political and a faggot. 'My friends and I are making it up each day we live. That's something.'

Robin climbs out the window onto the fire escape to think and be alone. Barnaby and Bruce, Barnaby's sometime boy-friend, are already there, smoking a joint.

"They are the only ones left to trust in this country," Barnaby says, as smoke slowly leaves his mouth, pointing to two drunks sleeping in a doorway across the street. "They cannot be bought off. All the rest of us have our price. Mine happens to be quite high, but it is still a price. But they have chosen to leave, to be useless. Nothing could bring them back."

"A lifetime supply of booze and they'd spy for the FBI, kill for the CIA," Bruce asserts, refusing to believe in bums.

"They'd take the booze, promising everything, and doze off when the bottle was empty." Barnaby knows the drunks very well. Often he will pick one up and bring him home. It is usually a sexual disaster, but he does learn a lot about their lives and their heads.

"Can they really have no price? That would be truly amazing in this country where everyone is for sale."

"Look how much they have given up. No family, only a few drinking friends any of whom might disappear at any moment. No ties to anything we consider necessary to live."

"And they die like crazy, freezing to death in the winter, beaten up by thugs in the summer," Bruce argues.

"Freedom is not easy."

Bruce snorts. He was born a cynic. He has never been able

to believe in anything. He thinks even his friends are hypocrites, mild hypocrites compared to most of the world, but still their actions never live up to their stated opinions. This does not surprise him. Rather it confirms his notion that everyone is in it for themselves. Bruce is easy to love, but it is hard when he loves you back. He sees the world from such an angle that everything anyone does is suspect. It used to make Robin angry, but now he accepts it as one more valid view of the way the world works.

The joint is finished. Robin's melancholy has been pushed aside by contentment at being here with two old friends. "Nice art piece," he says. "I had no idea you knew so many people."

Barnaby slaps his arm, an affectionate gesture for him, and smiles.

"You brute."

"You love it."

"Not the way you love it."

Suddenly Maybellene sticks her head out the window. "Robin, Charlie's here. He's been hurt, come quickly."

Robin's stomach turns over. He tries to rise but his knees give out.

"Come on!" Barnaby is on his feet pulling Robin up. Robin lunges through the window, nearly falling. "Where is he?"

"Near the door." Maybellene takes his hand and leads him through the crowded living room. Robin spots Charlie. He is wearing the red beanie Robin crocheted for him and his tan trenchcoat. He is holding something to his nose. His eye is swelling up and turning black. Robin moves across the floor in a panic. Charlie sees him and reaches out to him. They collapse into each other's arms. Charlie is shaking. Robin holds him for a minute, rubbing his back, kissing his neck, near tears.

"Wait, I'll bleed all over you. My nose. It won't stop."

Robin breaks the hug, realizing at once that Charlie is totally drunk.

"Honey, what happened?"

Charlie looks at him so pitifully that tears fall out of

Robin's eyes.

"I tried. I hurt one of them I'm sure. I tried. I was good. I was strong. I fought back. I only ran later. I did try." He begins to sob and Robin takes him back into his arms.

"Here, put this on your eye. It'll make it feel better." Rosa has wrapped some ice cubes in a towel. "Are you hurt? Is anything broken?" Rosa asks. Robin is recovering and feeling stupid for not asking first.

"I don't think so." Rosa gently touches Charlie's body here and there. "No, really, I'm O.K. Oh, the ice feels good. Thanks so much."

"What happened to you?" Robin is finally composed enough to ask, though he doesn't really want to know. He fights his own street paranoia all the time. He is determined not to let fear keep him at home. He will not be made a prisoner in his own house, afraid to venture out. Yet each new attack is more fuel for his fear. He doesn't see well at night and he is not a fast runner, so he feels vulnerable to random violence. And he is. One night he and Bruce and Barnaby were walking on Bleecker Street holding hands and laughing, stoned, when some kids threw an empty wire trash can at them and began to chase them down the street yelling "faggot" at them. Robin's glasses flew off and when he stopped to get them he couldn't see where they were. Barnaby grabbed his arm and pulled him into a store for safety. Later he found his glasses. They had been run over by a car.

"I was putting up posters..."

"By yourself?"

"Well, after the show ended, Jim and I went drinking and then it got late. He had to leave and we hadn't done any yet, so I went out to do some. Just a few. I really didn't feel like it. I wanted to come here and be with you. So I figured I'd walk here and put them up on the way and that's what I did. Across on Bleecker Street and then down Second and after I crossed Houston I was putting up the last one and these three kids..."

"White, black, Spanish?"

"They weren't blacks or Spanish. Italian maybe. They were suddenly right next to me asking to see the poster."

"Not exactly a subtle poster."

"And they started saying stuff, you know the usual, 'Is this a queer show?' 'Are you queer?' So I started talking..."

"Saying yes?" Robin asks astonished.

"Well, yes," Charlie answers with a hint of defensiveness in his clear blue eyes. "It seemed O.K. But then they began asking what I liked to do. 'You suck cock?' 'You like your ass fucked?' I knew then, just by their tone, that things were about to get ugly. Then one of them hit me on the arm, sort of shoved me and I shoved him back but I knew I had to get out of there. I guess they were caught off guard when I started hitting..."

"They never expect queers to fight back," sneers Rosa.

"...and so they didn't come after me when I ran. I ran all the way here."

"They might still be out there. We should tell everyone to leave here in groups. I'll spread the word," says Maybellene as she moves off, cool and efficient, into the crowd.

"They should all be killed."

"Let's go look for them and knock the shit out of them," says Ruby, excited at the thought of challenging these straight, violent men.

"Not me. I'd rather shoot them. They don't deserve to live."

"Rosa," exclaims Emma, her sense of justice outraged, "how can you say that? They are people too. Fucked up and oppressed like everyone else."

"They are scum. Violent, hate-filled good-for-nothings. Terrifying people. They should die." Rosa had been caught by a gang of young toughs on a San Francisco bus. They had beaten him unconscious while the other passengers looked on. In that moment of pain and humiliation he had killed his gentle hippie pacifism and given birth to a rage that wanted revenge.

"How's your nose doing?"

"I think it's stopped. I did try though. I really did."

"You did great," says Ruby proudly and puts his arm around Charlie. Charlie begins to cry. "Just cry. It's good for you."

"I wish you'd been there."

"Me too. It would have been great."

"We could have done it. I just couldn't do it alone."

"Of course you couldn't."

Robin puts his arms around Ruby and Charlie, lays his head on Charlie's shoulder and weeps softly. How afraid Charlie had been of New York. He had only moved here because he fell in love with Robin and Robin had to be here to work. He was a small-town boy. He liked to know who everybody was and what their story was. It made him feel safe. He felt like he had a place. New York had overwhelmed him, unnerved him. For the first six months he barely left the apartment. He didn't know how to make friends, how to choose from among all these thousands of strangers. He was afraid on the streets. For a month or so he refused to walk on the street with Robin because Robin couldn't run fast enough in case anything happened. But in the last year he began to feel stronger, more confident. 'And now he's fighting back,' thinks Robin, proud in a way, not of the fighting which he abhors, but of Charlie's new strength.

"What's that smell?" Charlie gasps.

"Just dead fish in the bathtub." It had become part of the place and hardly anyone noticed it anymore. A siren suddenly flashes through the apartment. They all jump.

"What's that?"

"The music."

"Where were they when I needed them?"

"They are only on records these days. You don't think they'd go out on these streets in person, do you?"

The three men untangle themselves. Ruby gives Charlie a Quaalude and someone passes him a glass of wine and a joint.

"The rewards to the conquering hero," someone shouts from the crowded room.

"More like some crumbs for the survivor," retorts Bruce angrily.

The numbness that Robin had so carefully cultivated has vanished. 'I'm completely sober,' he thinks morosely. Before he can move, Maybellene hands him a drink and winks a sly one. "Here's to numbness," she says.

"You mean the promise of numbness."

"Promise them anything but give them numbness," Rosa chimes in cheerily. They all click their glasses and drink to that.

5

EXPLORING NUMBNESS

"My coat's missing," Rosa yells, pouring through the remains in the closet.

"It must be there. Who would want *that* rag?" Bruce joins him in the search.

"Which one is it?"

"My fur."

"The one that looks like it was in too many cat fights before it became a coat?"

"The same."

"It must have cost you at least a dollar at a fine store someplace."

"Three fifty, to be exact," Rosa answers with a pout.

"Wear this." Barnaby throws him an old thick sweater.

"What about the fish?" Robin wonders out loud to no one in particular. Once he believed that Charlie was all right he had pursued a rigorous regime of consuming and now it was paying off. He might be anywhere and he could care less.

"I'll put them in a garbage bag and leave them on the street. Maybe they'll make a few rats sick."

Engulfed in a putrid fish smell, they stumble down the creaking, shaking stairs to the street. A light, gritty rain falls. They hardly notice. They clutch tightly to each other and walk as quickly as they can manage to the Terminal Bar.

Gloria Gaynor is screaming "I will survive" from the pink and blue jukebox. They throw their coats off and join her, stomping around the bar greeting everyone they know and some they don't know. When the record stops, Robin hears himself screaming, "Sex, drugs and rock 'n' roll," something he never says. Thinking he should be embarrassed, he tries to pretend he is by retreating sheepishly to a barstool next to Bruce.

"That's it. Sex, drugs and rock 'n' roll. Great. It sounds like something to live for," Bruce says as facetiously as he can manage. Yet pleasure is the one thing Bruce can understand, though he doesn't believe in it. Pleasure is far too transitory, too uncertain, too liable to turn sour too quickly to be believed in. But the concreteness of pleasure makes it possible for Bruce to take it seriously. Certainly more seriously than he can take radical talk or local art or assertions of love. He only objects when his lovers interrupt his pleasure. He doesn't miss "I love you" when it's no longer said because he never knows what it means anyway. But he knows at once what "I don't want to suck your cock anymore" means. 'Talk is cheap, but a tongue in the asshole is right now,' he often thinks. He doesn't understand why anyone would say no when the sex is still hot. He is nervous about Barnaby, who he is sleeping with these days, because he thinks Barnaby might do just that. Barnaby lives in his head and Bruce knows that those are the people who always fuck up pleasure. They always find some reason why it wouldn't be a good idea if we licked each other's balls right now. He realizes that he can say "sex, drugs and rock 'n' roll" with certainly more conviction than Robin can and turns to Robin and smiles.

Robin relaxes on his stool. Emma leans against him for support. Her eyes are half closed, her lips move in slow, circular motions as a small smile crosses her face. She speaks slowly, enunciating each word, carefully feeling how it sounds. "We have moved directly from innocence to decadence."

Maybellene jerks her head up trying to look intelligent but is unable to keep her eyes from crossing. "And what did we miss?"

"Maturity, I guess." Emma is uncertain.

"Oh, like our parents. I hadn't noticed that we'd missed that one. I feel more like my mother every day."

"They are hardly mature," Emma insists, clutching the bar with her hand. "They are total innocents. They live completely

40

in a dream world. My mother thinks the people on the soaps are real and my father thinks the seven o'clock news is the truth."

"My father thinks you can live on Social Security."

"Did he ever try it?"

"Of course not."

"It's good we stopped being innocent and moved right along, skipping all those middle stages, right into decadence. It seems like the most sensible place to be."

"If this is decadence, then I'm disappointed." From a slouch, Maybellene raises her body up to full height. "I thought it would have more pizazz to it." Her body starts to sway and she is nearly singing. "I thought it would be laced with scintillation, touched with hints of evil, vibrating with the forbidden. But instead it's being queer and stoned in a sleazy bar. I thought decadence would be more glamorous than this."

"But darling, everything we do is glamorous." Emma moves away from the bar grabbing Maybellene's hand. "Let's play pool."

Robin is startled out of a semi-trance when Emma stops leaning on him. He looks around to remember where he is and notices, through barely open eyes, Charlie and Ruby walking with their arms around each other into the toilet. When they close the door behind themselves, Robin leaves his stool and walks to the greasy windows to pretend to stare out at the street. 'Shit,' he thinks. When he and Charlie are in the bar together, which isn't that often, they usually pay only minimal attention to each other. It is part of their attempt to give each other plenty of space. 'But there are limits,' Robin thinks fiercely, knowing that actually there are no limits unless they define them. "Do not bring someone home to have sex if the other person is there." That was a limit they set up early and easily. Yet even that rule was once broken when Robin arrived home to find Charlie fucking with some stranger on the living room floor. Charlie apologized with a giggle and continued; Robin retreated to the bedroom, turned the radio up loud, took a pill and went to sleep. 'Are there any other rules?' He can't think of any others. 'I don't care what they do, but why do they have to do it in front of me?' He wants to cry but he can't. 'They could have included me.'

He is near self-pity when he hears Rosa scream, "It was so avant I nearly threw up. I prefer my art hanging on the walls rather than floating in the bathtub."

Barnaby stumbles into Robin, puts his arm around his shoulder and squeezes.

"I'm going home," Robin announces.

"They won't even remember doing it tomorrow."

"But I will, I promise." Robin believes that to keep a relationship going, someone has to get mad, or at least pout when something goes wrong. "Give me a kiss." It is a long, nearly passionate one.

Barnaby releases Robin and smiles at him. "Tomorrow will bring another reality," he says as his eyeballs make a full circle in their sockets. Robin grabs his coat and lunges out the door.

Barnaby suddenly must hear if any sounds are coming from the toilet. He points his nose in its direction, but his knees shake, his hands grab the nearest stranger for support and his feet move him to the bench, where he crumples in a heap.

The toilet is not generating much heat. Charlie and Robin are in that drunken place where desire is far greater than ability. Charlie pushes Ruby against the wall and manages to get his pants down. He plops on his knees and begins to suck the limp cock. Ruby closes his eyes and imagines what pleasure he is getting. It takes more skill than they can summon to change positions so they continue until loud knocks on the door penetrate their fog.

Ruby collects his pants and Charlie collects his wits. It has just occurred to him that Robin is in the bar and his behavior, if noticed, might cause some small ripples in the surface of their domesticity. He cannot be sure, though. At first he was puzzled by the apparent randomness of Robin's jealousy. He might go to the baths, get fucked all night long, come home and Robin would act as if he had just come from the supermarket. Or he might harmlessly flirt with a cute actor over drinks after a play in front of Robin and Robin would sulk for a week. Slowly, he realized that it was not what he did, but where he did it. He had no idea how Robin might feel about him and Ruby but he had a feeling it might not be good. They had never had sex together before, though calling what just happened sex seems to him to be stretching a point.

'But I fought a good fight tonight and I deserved a reward,' he thinks as he plunges out of the toilet. Charlie quickly looks for Robin but does not see him. Relieved, he takes Ruby's hand and pulls him into a dark corner. "Let's make out."

Since Charlie started the whole encounter, Ruby feels relieved of all responsibility. Besides, Robin would not be angry at him. Robin expects him to act like a whore. And Ruby, who loves the role, obliges him as often as possible.

Ruby and Charlie sit on a bench against the wall near the pool table. It runs halfway around the room. The radiators are directly under the bench, so it is the coziest place in the bar. Making out as best they can, Ruby suddenly realizes that the left leg of his pants is wet. 'Fuck. What did I do?' Surreptitiously he checks his crotch. Not wet. The bench. Very wet. As he slides his hand along the bench it gets wetter. Abruptly he jumps up, cursing. Several feet away sits Barnaby with his arm around Bruce and a smile on his face so innocent that Ruby knows at once who the source is.

"Oh, no, this bottle of beer just fell over and spilled," Barnaby mockingly moans. Barnaby starts to brush off Ruby's pants with a solicitous gesture. Ruby slaps his hand away.

"Giving much tough guy, huh?" Barnaby shoves Ruby hard enough to send him careening backwards until he falls into the middle of the pool table. Maybellene has just missed the ball for the third straight time and she is pissed off. Balls scatter over the table and onto the floor.

"Fucking men. We can't even have a quiet game of pool without you bums..." Maybellene shouts as she pokes Ruby with her pool cue. Ruby recovers his balance but not his cool. He lunges back across the room at Barnaby but stumbles and falls into his arms.

"Come to give mama a kiss? How sweet." Ruby looks up at Barnaby's face. His vision is filled with nose. His mind goes blank as he plants his teeth into Barnaby's nose. Barnaby screams, hits him hard in the stomach and Ruby collapses onto the floor. Barnaby runs to the toilet to examine his nose while Charlie and Bruce pick Ruby up and sit him on a dry spot on the bench.

"You boys are having quite an evening for yourselves," says Maybellene snidely from the floor where she is trying to catch a ball which won't stop rolling. Emma, disgusted, is balancing herself with the aid of her pool cue. "It's like going out with a bunch of hit men for the Mafia."

"So refined, so high class..." Maybellene continues crawling among the old cigarette butts, chasing another ball.

Bruce turns Ruby towards him and slaps him hard across the face. Ruby opens his eyes and smiles.

Barnaby returns with a piece of toilet paper stuck to his nose. He gives Ruby a look of death and settles down to be comforted by Bruce, who begins kissing his face and stroking his arms. Ruby and Charlie return to smooching. Emma weaves her way to the bench, stands in front of them and says loudly, "I see all that violence got you boys hot."

At that moment the lights in the bar are turned up. They all squint and blink and moan.

"It's all over but the gossip," Maybellene declares.

They stumble out into the gritty air.

The next day, as the phones ring all over the Lower East Side, the evening is judged a great success. The art piece was flawless and the bar perfect. They deplore quiet nights at the bar. Without a scandal or two, without some minor uproar or the possibility of it, they feel cheated. They love what the world so quaintly calls infidelities and also public sex and social faux pas and indelicate language and raunchy stories. They would never sacrifice their politics for an amusing story, but they would sacrifice nearly anything else and often do.

6

BAN THE BUMS

Barnaby opens his eyes a crack to look at the clock. It says ten o'clock. He rolls over, pulling the covers over his head. A flash suddenly explodes in his mind. 'I've lost a day. It's not tomorrow. It's the day after tomorrow.' He had unplugged the phone. He did not want to hear the verdict on the art piece, nor did he want to hear about what had actually happened. He would remember enough. He always remembered enough. 'If I did miss a day then I'm supposed to be at work.' He reaches for the phone, plugs it in and calls work. His supervisor, a jolly dyke from Oklahoma, answers.

"I'm too sick to code today."

"What else is new?" She laughs at her little joke. "Your party was great. I met some weird people there and you know how soft I am for weirdos."

"Glad you liked it. I'll see you tomorrow." He lies on the bed until he begins to feel his mind and body reuniting. Lenin arouses himself from a nap in the corner and begins running from one end of the apartment to the other, his way of saying "I'm hungry." Barnaby stretches his arm out, finds a box of Friskies and pours more than he intends on the floor. Lenin crunches away happily.

With his arm outside the covers, Barnaby realizes that the heat is off again. Barnaby closes his eyes as he carefully lays his head against the pillow. 'You won't get depressed today,' he tells himself firmly. 'If you insist on living in a half-abandoned building, you have to expect the heat to go off now and then.' This approach usually does not work. Being by nature rebellious and defiant, he cannot bear to follow even his own orders. 'That's why my life is shaped so strangely. Whatever I order myself to do is exactly what I'm not going to do.'

'So get depressed. Ruin another day.'

'I will, dammit, if I want to.'

'Go ahead. Wallow in it. Why don't you make a list of everything that is wrong?'

'That's an idea.' He moans, rubs his crotch and actually manages to move his mouth into a smile. He likes being perverse and contrary. He thinks it makes him mysterious. He knows it makes him unpredictable. The bourgeois life of constancy and fixed purpose has always struck him as monstrously boring.

He wraps a blanket around himself and gets up. He begins to clean up the leftovers from the art piece but loses patience quickly. 'I'll abandon the apartment for now,' he thinks as he begins selecting an outfit for the streets.

Barnaby wears only black, a decision made originally to simplify getting dressed. When Robin pointed out to him that he looked like an anarchist flag, he knew he had made the right decision. Yet it did not make getting dressed any easier. After an hour of throwing black clothes all over his bedroom he is finally ready to visit the outside.

He remembers his nose and scurries to the bathroom to examine it. A small scab is the only evidence left. 'I must remember not to forget about this,' he thinks.

Trying to imagine what it was like to be black in Watts during the riot, he steps onto the street. The day is overcast with a greenish brown haze, and cold. Two of his favorite bums are huddled in a doorway across from his building, drinking a pint.

"Hey, brother, got a cigarette?" They know enough not to ask him for money since he needs all he can earn just to keep himself high.

"Sure. How you doin' today?"

"O.K., man." They each take a cigarette. "And a light?" Barnaby, finishing the ritual, lights each cigarette. "The fucking Shelter is too crowded. We had to sleep on the floor last night and some bastard pissed all over us."

"We were lucky to get in at all. About twenty guys were

sleeping on the steps outside 'cause there ain't no room inside and those motherfuckers hung out the upstairs window and poured hot water all over them."

Barnaby's stomach flips. "Why?"

"To get them to leave, I reckon."

"Naw," the other drunk protests. "Probably did it just to watch those guys squirm. Those motherfuckers who run that place are shit holes."

"What happened to them?"

"Don't know. Probably froze to death last night."

"Oh, it was all psychos anyway." The state, in a move to save money, had recently released everyone who could walk from their mental hospitals onto the streets. Many had come into the neighborhood since the Men's Shelter is one of the few free places to stay in all of Manhattan. The drunks are often frightened now. Their stable, predictable world is being shattered by men who live by different rules.

"How 'bout another cigarette to get us through?"

"Sure. Take care." Barnaby begins walking up Second Avenue. The fresh air, such as it is, wakes him up. He notices as he walks that he is so awake that he is looking into all the men's faces as he passes. He likes it best when he is oblivious to men passing him. Everyone is bundled up against the cold so all he can see are pairs of eyes staring out at him. But for cruising, the eyes are sufficient. He suddenly feels horny. 'Shit, I should've jerked off this morning or asked Bruce home after the bar. Oh, but that was two nights ago.'

His lust, a slow but steady thing, has come to seem like a burden to him. He has begun to realize that his politics are pushing him into a completely untenable position. He hates men. They are violent, competitive and destructive. Yet he is a faggot and so loves men. It is a quandary for him. Phallic worship has brought misery to the race, yet he loves cocks. Hating maleness makes being a faggot absurd. He can still be charmed by a man, or, more honestly, still get hot over a man. But lately he finds that each man he meets will reveal quickly, very quickly, some strong male attitude and his mind will force him to withdraw, even be nasty. 'How can I suck someone off who repels me when I talk to him? How can I give pleasure to violent men? Maybe I should only sleep with drag queens. They are the only ones who have stepped outside of the patriarchy. But I never meet any drag queens anymore. I must ask Rosa where they've all gone.'

He figures he should have been a dyke. Then his politics and his sex life would fit nicely together. But he isn't. Could he love men and hate maleness? Could he love cock and hate the patriarchy? 'Others seem able to bring this one off. Maybe they just don't think about it. I probably think too much. I bring these problems on myself. Maybe I've just made this up to torment myself. Or maybe I'm too butch. Maybe I'm repelled by myself. I need sissy lessons. I need to de-man myself, rip maleness out of my own psyche and then I could suck cock with a clear conscience.' He once suggested to Robin that he should write a book entitled *How to Become a Queen and Lose Twenty Pounds on Your Lunch Hour*. He figured it would help people like him and sell like crazy. "That's easy," Robin had answered. "Just sit in a tearoom on your lunch hour every day for two months and do nothing but suck cock."

Suddenly, Barnaby notices that the sidewalks are clean. There is not a rotting orange peel or an empty beer can to be seen. Such a sight makes him nervous. 'I've come too far,' he thinks as he turns around and heads quickly back down Second Avenue.

He walks by a newsstand catching a headline. "200 Tons of Marijuana Seized." 'Shit. That should drive the price right up. At least there'll be dope around once the cops start unloading the stuff,' he reassures himself.

At Fourteenth Street he sees someone who looks like a drag queen. 'I'll cruise him.' As he tilts his head preparing to give a friendly smile, the person whisks by him without a glance. 'Maybe it wasn't a drag queen after all. I don't know if I can tell anymore.'

Coming to Third Street, he decides to walk by the Men's Shelter and check on the boiling water story. Turning the corner off Second Avenue, he is amazed to see people walking in front of the Shelter carrying signs. He hurries down the street until he is close enough to read them. "Bums out of the Neighborhood." "Shut the Shelter Down." "Make Third Street Safe." The pickets, about fifty of them, are all white and middle-aged, highly scrubbed and neatly dressed, members of the old, solid working class who have lived in the neighborhood forever. They march in a circle yelling obscenities at the few drunks unfortunate enough to be on the street. Cops surround them, protecting them from contact with the scum.

In a panic, Barnaby runs to Maybellene's apartment which is directly across the street from the Shelter. He rings the bell and waits. He rings again frantically. Finally, the buzzer sounds and he dashes up the stairs.

The door is ajar. Maybellene is hiding under the covers. "The goddamn heat's off again. What a way to start the day." Susan B. is batting a cockroach across the kitchen floor.

"Maybellene, there's a demonstration in front of the Shelter."

"What? They don't have heat either? Let's go join them."

"No, not that kind of demonstration. One sign says, 'Bums out of the Neighborhood.'"

"Bums out of the neighborhood? My God, that's us."

"Another says, 'Make Third Street Safe.'"

"Safe for who?"

"That's the point. If these bums go we all are finished, including those people who are picketing. Without them lying around on the street, looking obscene and broken, making people feel uncomfortable, the middle class will move right in. The bums force people to remember something about reality and mortality which most people spend their lives trying to hide from or forget."

"If the bums are forced out, the rents will go up. Don't these people know that? What should we do?"

51

"I don't know." He sighs as he collapses across Maybellene's bed. She reaches her arm out from under the covers and hands him a joint. "When in doubt, get stoned," she advises. Susan B., smelling the smoke, bounds onto the bed. "Let's have our own demonstration," she suggests, taking the joint back.

"Keep the bums in the neighborhood."

"Declare next week 'National Bum Week.'"

"Take a bum to lunch."

"Take a bum to bed."

"The bum you pass might be your father." They start giggling.

"I'll make flyers and we can put them up around here."

"Perfect," Maybellene says, feeling very much better. "Another art piece." She sees her whole life as a long succession of art pieces. It's why it takes her so long to get dressed to go anyplace. Art pieces require, at least, a correct outfit. It's also why she and Barnaby are such good friends. They met in a dance class run by a conceptual artist who didn't care if they could move their bodies as long as everyone placed themselves in an artistic arrangement in the room. Their teacher seemed to make so little out of so much that they figured they could make art also.

"Hand me something warm to wear and I'll make some coffee."

Barnaby finds a red wool sweater and a pair of black toreador pants. She dresses under the covers.

Maybellene walks to the kitchen and stares out of the window. Her kitchen faces the back, and across a small space she has a view of twenty different apartments. "Ah!" she screams suddenly. "There she is."

"Who?" Barnaby is on his feet in a bound, sending Susan B. flying off the bed.

"Oh, God. My cunt is twitching. Maybe she lives there. Oh, no. I'll die."

"Who? Where?"

"Away from the window," Maybellene orders. "She might see you. A man in my apartment. It could ruin it all before it begins." Maybellene dashes to the closet, rips off her clothes, frantically rummages through her stuff until she finds a black jersey blouse, cut low in the front, and a pair of red torn jeans. She brushes her short, stripped white hair straight up and dashes back to the window to lean casually on the sill. "You stay there in the corner."

"Do I know this goddess who has gotten you wet between the legs?"

"She was in the bar last night. Pink and white hair. Short. Very butch. Had her cigarettes rolled in the arm of her T-shirt. You couldn't miss her."

"I wasn't in the bar last night."

"You weren't? Was I? Maybe it wasn't last night. I'm losing track of the days. Where were you?"

"Asleep, I think. Who is she?"

"I wasn't introduced. But she had a heavy Brooklyn accent which in itself was enough to make my twat twitter."

Over coffee and another joint they map their strategy for National Bum Week, while Maybellene walks casually by the window every few seconds. Finally the woman notices her and waves. Maybellene waves back.

"So who cares if the heat's off, my head is three times too big and throbbing and they are trying to get rid of the bums. I may get laid this year."

Getting laid is not a simple matter for Maybellene. Until she was twenty-five she had only her own fingers for company. The thought of doing it with a man bored her. The thought of doing it with a woman did not enter her mind. She would have been a nun except that she could never bring herself to worship pain and sacrifice.

One night she unthinkingly walked into the Green Tulip. She refused to notice for the first hour that there were no men present. But she became so relaxed that she looked around for the reason and the reason flashed through her mind. So she started going every night, not talking to anyone, just letting herself feel secure and warm. As the months went by, she started saying to herself, 'So you must be a dyke.' The thought excited her.

One night a woman, small, young, with a crew cut, asked her home. Maybellene accepted. As they walked to the woman's apartment on Grove Street, Maybellene began to become unglued. 'I have to tell her.'

"This is my first time," she blurted out, interrupting a discourse on the impossibility of men.

"You mean I got a virgin?"

"I guess that's it."

"Great. It's easy." She took Maybellene's hand and squeezed it. "We'll go real slow."

Maybellene had decided not to go at all, but they were already walking through the door to the apartment.

The apartment was empty, except for a mattress on the floor, some pillows scattered around, and candles. Maybellene immediately lay down on the bed, closed her eyes, and waited, for what she wasn't sure.

The other woman lay down next to her and whispered, "Whatever you want to do is lovely."

Maybellene knew at once. "I want to suck your tits. Just that for now."

"Far out."

And for the next couple of hours Maybellene made love to the woman's tits, feeling more relaxed, more child-like and secure and more horny than she could ever remember feeling. She finally fell asleep.

In the morning they made love in a way that Maybellene thought must be more like what dykes usually do in bed.

Since then she has been Dottie Dyke for days. Since then she's known where her tongue belongs. The problem now is finding a woman to do it with. She isn't shy anymore or even afraid. She is just very fussy. She is lucky if she meets a couple of women a year she wants to make love with. She laments her unexpectedly rigid standards.

"When I came out," she once told Emma, "I assumed I'd be a complete slut. Once I got started at it. But it has worked out differently."

"You talk like a slut," Emma said, trying to reassure her.

"Yeah, big talk. No action."

Barnaby slowly rises from his chair, takes a step, and brings the point of his left black boot down on a cockroach. "One down and three million to go." Susan B. runs over to examine the corpse, sniffs and walks away disgusted. Barnaby wipes it up with his finger and washes it down the drain. "I wonder if they have cockroaches in nuclear power plants."

"I'm sure. They must. They thrive on all our garbage. They've probably already mutated a new line that just loves radioactive waste."

"The radioactive cockroach."

Barnaby wanders into the bedroom and looks out the window at the Shelter. "They've gone home. I guess it is safe to go out. I'm going home and make some flyers. I think I'll call it 'Save Our Bums, Save Ourselves.'"

"And I'm going to lounge by this window until I can figure out how to get that girl across this courtyard and into my bed."

7

THE LIMOUSINES ARE WAITING

Two nights later, Barnaby walks into the bar with firm resolve. He knows he'll get attitude from a group of Trotskyites who hang out at one end of the bar who think anything short of total revolution is a waste of time and he figures he'll get indifference from the old-timer drunks who hang out at the other end. The dykes might be up for it, especially since he has included the local bag ladies in his call for the protection of the undesirables. In fact, he has included everyone, titling the poster "We Are All Bums In America." He wanted to spell it Amerika, with a *k*, but he feared people would dish him for being so sixties.

He walks around the nearly empty bar and hands each person his leaflet. The bar looks like the Public Library Reading Room when Robin dashes in.

"Barnaby, there are limousines in the neighborhood," he gasps.

"What?" Barnaby does not grasp the magnitude of this new revelation.

"Four of them. I saw them. Parked right on Second Avenue. Long black ones with drivers wearing uniforms. Right on Second Avenue. The nerve!" Robin is so scandalized that he runs immediately to the bar for a drink. Barnaby follows.

"What does it mean?"

"What does it mean? I don't know exactly, but it can't be good. That the ruling class would dare to show themselves so blatantly in our neighborhood—well, it must mean something."

"Maybe they'll go away."

"But not before they do some damage, I'm sure. Right now

they're probably buying up half the neighborhood to convert it to co-ops for rich people or making some deal with some sleazy politician to steal even more money from us. They aren't even afraid of us. They are advertising their presence."

Barnaby realizes the seriousness of the situation. "Maybe we ought to steal their hubcaps. At the very least."

"Put sugar in their gas tanks. I hear that works."

"Tacks under their tires. That would stop them."

Having run out of tactics, Robin picks up a flyer. "Our demonstration comes in the nick of time. With those limousines out there you can bet the bums and bag ladies, as well as the rest of us, are under attack. Looks good."

A Trot walks up and asks Barnaby if he has gotten a permit.

"For what?"

"For this action."

"No. We'll take them by surprise."

"But you gotta have a permit or the cops will stop it."

"Great. It'll be good press."

"Provocateur," he mutters as he walks back to his cronies.

"Barnaby, you'll never organize anyone by giving them attitude."

"It is better to give attitude than to receive it."

"Always."

"They're just nervous about getting arrested. What kind of radical is that anyway?"

"I haven't been arrested since, when?" Robin thinks. "1968, I guess, eleven years ago."

"Well, it's about time."

Rosa enters, his eyes darting around until he spots them. He saunters over, flops onto a stool and begins: "I went to the West Village last night in search of some sex. My dears, it is worse than we thought. I could not tell one man from another."

"We all look alike with our clothes off," Barnaby says sarcastically.

"No. They all had their clothes on."

"That's how they like it there."

"To look exactly like each other?"

"It makes them feel a part of something."

"It helps them recognize each other."

"What is the point of going through all the trouble it takes to become a faggot and then end up looking like everyone else?"

"It's simpler," Robin explains, refusing to get upset about something they have known about for years. "This look is hot. Look this way and everyone will think you're hot. Life is difficult enough without having to figure out what is going to turn each person on."

"Well, I think it is oppressive and silly. I am announcing, as of this moment, a sexual boycott of clones."

"Rosa, I think it is extreme to give up clones and romance in the same week. You'll have to stay home a lot."

"Did you score, as they say there?"

"I did," Rosa smiles. "He said I looked exotic."

"He meant you looked 'out-of-town.'"

"Not at all. He thought I was foreign."

"Did you tell him you were from the distant Lower East Side?"

"I did and he said that was foreign enough for him."

"Did he take you home?"

"Of course not. He took me to his local bar which had a back room and we did it there. They don't do it in beds anymore over there, I hear."

"Saves cleaning the sheets."

"Prevents robberies."

In the midst of the dishing, Barnaby hands Rosa a flyer. "Oh, a demonstration. How sixties. But why not something more gay?"

"There are gay bums," Barnaby answers firmly.

"You ought to know. You've slept with enough of them."

"Not that many. They always end up getting all my money out of me, so I can't do it too often."

"Are they good in bed?" Rosa is after the juice.

"Did you ever know a drunk who was a good lay?"

"You're not too bad," Robin snickers.

"You can remember?" Barnaby asks.

"Actually, not that well." Robin and Barnaby always have sex when they are both smashed on Quaaludes or drunk. It always seems nice the next day, but it is difficult to remember the exact details about who put what where. Robin is always sore afterwards so he knows the sex is not the gentlest and the last time his ass hurt, so he figured Barnaby must have fucked him.

"Demonstrations are a bit tired. You have to admit." Rosa is about to go into his disillusioned radical routine. "They didn't end the war or bring racial equality, did they?" Rosa is nearly gloating.

"You are into armed struggle now?" asks Robin sarcastically.

"Violence. It is all they understand. The other stuff just doesn't work." Rosa thinks of himself as a deeply political person, even though he has to admit, when pressed on the point, that he has never actually done anything himself. He managed a couple of Gay Pride marches in New York and a demonstration for the handicapped in San Francisco. He doesn't like demonstrations and he can't handle violence, so all his tough talk is just talk. When Robin calls him on his hypocrisy, Rosa becomes huffy and changes the subject.

"Armed struggle sounds great. Except they have all the guns. That's going to make the odds a trifle uneven."

"Guerrilla warfare is the only way to smash their power."

Robin moans, "Oh, no. It's back to the Catskills where we can pick off Eastern holy men and migrant farm workers from our secret caves."

Rosa puts on a big pout, turns, and orders a drink. By the time he gets it, he has a reply. "So there we'll be and two hundred crazed men will dash out of the Men's Shelter to panhandle us. Better bring lots of spare change."

"So you're not coming?"

"Of course I'm coming. I never miss a chance to dress up."

"Did you see the limousines?"

"I did. Who do we know who drives one of those things? I'd go out with him in a minute."

Getting exasperated, Robin snaps, "They do not belong to our friends, Rosa. Only rich people have limousines and chauffeurs," nearly embarrassed to be stating the obvious.

"Rosa," Barnaby whispers conspiratorially, "there's a man cruising you."

"Where, Who?" Rosa's head swivels nearly full circle.

"Over there." Barnaby indicates with his eyes a small black man in a purple T-shirt, leaning against the jukebox.

"Oh, my. I'm definitely ready for him. Do you think I should tell him I've given up romance?"

"It seems a little premature."

"But I don't want to lead him on."

"Maybe you should see if he wants to be led on first."

"Did you tell the one last night you're off romance?"

"Of course. Oh, what should I do? I'm coming unglued."

"Try to relax your nerves and then go play the jukebox and say hello. This is a friendly bar."

Rosa takes a deep breath, a huge drag on a joint, a gulp from his drink, and strolls, in a manner he considers casual, over to the man.

"For someone who's given up romance, he sure moves fast."

"If he plays Patti Smith again, I'm leaving the bar."

Patti Smith comes out of the speakers.

"After this drink." They stand engulfed in sound.

"No one ever cruises me here," Robin notes with slight disappointment.

"You've got to show it off more. Let them know you're ready," Barnaby advises.

"But I'm not ready. I must give off heavy keep-your-mouth-to-yourself vibes."

"Me too, I never want them to talk. I'm usually turned off by the second sentence," Barnaby confesses.

Two dykes walk up to them. "We'll be there. Any special outfits required?"

"Dress so you can fade into the crowd if the cops come."

"That should be easy enough." They stroll arm in arm out the door.

Emma bounds through the door, crashing into the two women leaving. She stops to apologize and then leaps to the bar. She is wearing a white tailored blouse with a string black tie, a plaid skirt and knee-length argyle socks with saddle shoes.

"I just got off work," she announces with a sigh of relief.

"You have a new job as a cheerleader?"

"I've been promoted to running the cash register." She smiles. They all understand at once. She lifts up her skirt slightly and money can be seen sticking very slightly out of the tops of her socks. She reaches down and pulls out a twenty. "Drinks are on me." She pulls out a ten and several ones. She reaches into her left shoe for another ten and into her right shoe for a few singles. The pocket of her blouse gives up a five and her cleavage another twenty. "Bras come in handy. Not bad, huh?"

"Was there anything left in the cash drawer?"

"Plenty. The outfit is not perfected yet, but it's not half bad for a beginner, huh?"

"Or for a chickenshit."

"You don't have to be brave. Just clever. As long as all your totals match."

"So you got promoted?"

"It's only temporary. The cashier got sick. But it came just in time. I didn't have the money for rent yet. Now I can live in that cold, stinking, cockroach-crawling apartment for another month. Oh, let me see the flyer."

"Did you see the limo..." But before he can get the word out they hear glass shattering and people screaming. They are the people screaming.

"Hit the floor," a bartender yells and they fall down into the grime. Rosa and the other bartender rush from the back to the front door. Rosa is screaming. "Nazis! Fascists! Pigs!"

Robin clutches Emma and Barnaby. "Are we going to join Harvey Milk in homo heaven?" he asks plaintively.

"This may be homo heaven," Barnaby answers, trying to ignore his heart exploding.

"Call the cops."

"Dirty punks."

"Get up. They ran away." Rosa helps the three off the floor. One of the huge greasy windows facing the pool table is shattered. Glass fragments and split paper bags stuffed with this week's garbage, beer cans and old plaster cover the red felt pool table, the bench and the floor. A garbage can lies conspicuously on the floor.

"Is anybody hurt?"

"I just called the cops," one bartender says.

"Did anyone see them?" another bartender asks.

"Yeah," one of the Trots volunteers. "Looked like four young kids. They were at the curb and then they ran in different directions."

"Did you recognize anyone?"

"No."

"At least it wasn't a bomb."

Everyone goes back to his drink while the bartender begins cleaning up. The man in the purple T-shirt moves quickly out the door.

"Those creeps." Rosa is indignant. "They just ruined my sex life."

"At least for tonight."

"Isn't that what they wanted to do?" Robin asks. "They imagine us in here having orgies, stoned out on the most exotic drugs there are, drugs they haven't even heard of yet and they've got nothing. No sex, no drugs, only rock 'n' roll. If they can't have it, then we can't have it either."

"They should only come in here and see what a sedate bunch we are." Rosa runs to the shattered window and yells out, "Boys, there hasn't been an orgy in here in years." He trots back to them. "If they knew what they were missing, they'd miss it."

"It's those limousines. Just having them here makes those thugs think they can get away with anything," Robin says gloomily.

"And it looks like they have," Barnaby announces triumphantly. "Has anyone noticed any cops around yet?"

"Haven't seen them."

"Probably a shift change so no one's on duty."

"They're all too busy protecting the banks from getting robbed to bother with a queer bar."

"They have to change their drag from punk to cop. That way we won't recognize them when they come back," Emma says bitterly. "I think we should get out of here. I'm getting paranoid."

"Does the street look clear?"

"Yeah."

"Then let's make a run for it."

8

CONTRADICTIONS CAN SPOIL THE FUN

Robin wakes up with a foul taste in his mouth. He rolls over and bumps into Charlie, who opens his eyes, smiles and falls back to sleep. Robin remembers that he's forgotten to be upset about Charlie and Ruby in the toilet. 'It's a little late now,' he decides and rolls away from Charlie.

'I should call off my classes today. I need a rest from that place.' He begins playing with himself, then remembers he has an important meeting. It is about the schedule for the next semester. 'If I don't go, I'll end up with all eight o'clock in the morning classes, if I get any classes at all.' He has been a part-time college teacher for three years now. He gets the leftover classes, the ones the full-time faculty are too bored to teach. They keep promising him a full-time job, but the university is bankrupt so no one new can be hired. The pay is low, but it is a job.

He lies there trying to decide what he will talk about in "Marriage and the Family" today. When the head of the department, a noted heterosexual, had initially asked him to teach the course he had snorted, "In the interest of justice, I think they should both be destroyed."

The department head replied, "You seem to be on the right track." So he had agreed to teach the course.

When he told this story to Rosa, Rosa had said, "The breeders won't even defend their own institution. I thought it was the major thing they cared about after God and country."

"I guess they have lost the faith." They both agreed that this was a positive sign.

He decided to use the course to launch a major attack on both marriage and families, but he is finding it rather rough going since only two people in the entire class think that either institution, as we now know them, will last out the decade. And everyone appears to think that this is a positive development.

He watches Charlie sleep. When he starts to feel nostalgic for their past, he quietly slides out of bed and dresses.

He buys the *Times* to read on the subway, but when he gets on the train all the lights are out in his car. He heads for the next car, but it is dark also. With his body tense and his mind alert, he rides to South Ferry armed only with his newspaper.

The ferry to Staten Island is sunny and he sits on the top deck away from the crowds on the main deck. 'I'll do pornography today,' he is thinking when the ferry bangs into the wooden piles.

"The pilot must be drunk again," an old woman says, falling onto the bench next to him.

"Always."

"Somebody's going to get hurt one day."

"Probably be us."

'Heterosexual pornography is an expression of male sexuality, proof that men are obsessed with big cocks and find sexual stimulation in sadism,' he thinks walking into the meeting room. A woman in the department, another part-timer, is the only person there. They are friends, but powerless to make any decisions. They sit together with forms and information spread out before them, playing at planning the next semester's curriculum. Robin has brought tea in a Styrofoam cup and a jelly roll. He bites into the jelly roll and jelly drips out of it onto his pants. His colleague, a robust woman who eats all the time and is now sipping a large container of Coke and eating a butter-dripping bagel, does not comment on the dripping jelly. Robin tries to wipe it away with his fingers, but then another glob splashes onto the other leg of pants. His colleague talks on and on as she always does. Robin puts the jelly out of his mind to concentrate on her explanations of the intricacies of the curriculum. The jelly continues to drip. Onto his shirt and then, with a splat, onto the floor.

Robin leaves the meeting and goes directly to the bathroom to wash up. When he walks into class his pants and shirt are still wet. He heads for the desk and sits, low in his seat, behind it. They know by now that he is eccentric. Several people have commented on the fact that his socks never match. He shaves once a week, if he remembers. He carries a bag rather than a briefcase. He wears sneakers when the weather is good and a fur coat when it snows. He is always the worst dressed person in the room.

'I'll have to sit here for the whole period,' he thinks gloomily.

Suddenly someone is pushing a movie projector into the room and the students become excited. They love movies. Robin, forgetting the state of his clothes, rises up saying: "I didn't ask for a movie."

"What is it?" someone asks.

"Teaching circuitry to slow learners," the operator reads from his form.

"Definitely not for us," he informs the young man, who submissively turns around and leaves.

Everyone puts on their classroom faces—serious and blank—as Robin writes "Pornography" on the blackboard and then dashes back behind the desk. The front row perks up at once.

He is just finishing a discussion of penis size and aggression—"Small dicks make for big wars"—when the bell rings. Before he can finish his sentence, half the class is gone. An hour later he is still talking with a few students about dirty movies they have seen.

After one other class in which he describes in great detail the organization of Nazi death camps he leaves school. He is horny from all the sex talk and slightly terrified from the concentration camp talk, so he cruises the Staten Island Ferry men's room on the way home. It is mildly amusing though it stinks of ammonia and piss so badly that he can only stay in it for a few minutes at a time. Two men who apparently had the foresight to bring nose plugs provide the show for the others who dash in, watch, become overwhelmed by fumes and dash out for air.

Coming off the ferry, the wind is bitter and tears through him. He runs for the First Avenue bus, leaps on, pays his fare and sits down. After fifteen minutes the bus driver gives up trying to start it and tells them all to take another bus. The second bus runs, but the windows in the back do not close. Robin freezes in the front where all the passengers are crowded together.

The bus leaves him off at Fourteenth Street. He goes directly to a straight pornographic movie theater where he sucks someone off in the balcony. When he leaves he notices he has chewing gum all over the knees of his pants. 'Fuck. Queens can be so thoughtless. Who would leave gum on the floor of a dirty movie house? What am I going to say to Charlie? I'll deny everything. I'll abandon these pants. Charlie won't even notice. He won't even care. That's what hurts.' Mild anxiety grips his stomach as he races through the dark, cold streets for home.

Putting the key in the lock, he hears the phone ringing.

"Hello," he says, gasping for air.

"This is Emma. What's the matter?"

"Just breathless. How are you?"

"I'm trying to figure out whether to be a social worker, a schoolteacher or a waitress for the rest of my life."

"You're already a waitress."

"Yeah, and it sucks a dead moose."

That is one of Emma's favorite expressions and Robin has never been able to figure out what it means. "So it's either a schoolteacher or a social worker. That's easier."

"They both have their disadvantages, however."

"Oh?"

"Well, I know the middle class uses social work to keep the poor in line and I hate large groups of kids."

"So it's back to waitress. I thought you were on the cash drawer now."

"That ended after one shift. I think they might have been a tiny bit suspicious. All day I've been trying to imagine myself deciding who is and who is not fit for welfare. But I know I'd die a little bit every time I had to refuse somebody. Then I tried to imagine myself telling a bunch of teen-agers about the pleasure of reading Virginia Woolf but instead I kept seeing them booing me out of the classroom. But I'm tired of being a servant and waiting on people all the time. Yet the only alternative seems to be to become a boss. Aren't there any decent jobs left in America?"

"I'll think about it and see if I come up with any."

"So my future is as clouded as ever. Oh, look, let's go to the movies. Rosa wants to go."

"Great," Robin says, forgetting that he has just come from the movies. "What's playing?"

"*Trash* and *Desperate Living.*"

"Fab."

"It's in twenty minutes at the St. Marks."

"I'll meet you there."

Auden and Gloria are screaming so he feeds them. He walks around the apartment saying hello to the plants before he changes his pants, burying the gummy ones deep in a nearly full plastic garbage bag. He leaves Charlie a note, "Gone out," swallows half a Quaalude and leaves for the movies.

They buy popcorn and Cokes. The theater is crowded and noisy. The only three empty seats together are in the second row on the far left side. To see the screen they must bend their heads backwards and twist them to the side. The images appear elongated and grotesque. The popcorn is stale and the Cokes are flat. A man behind them begins to snore loudly. Three children wander up and down the aisle looking for their mother. Someone yells "Fire"and everyone laughs. When Rosa's seat breaks, sending him to the floor, they decide to leave.

"That was a bummer," Emma says as they hurry down a

cold, garbage-strewn Second Avenue. The wind is blowing hard into their faces. Emma is attacked by a flying newspaper. She defends herself with great skill. A cardboard box smacks Rosa's legs. He kicks it, sending it bounding into the street where a car hits it.

"Fucking cold for March," Robin mutters as a cloud of grit flies by their heads. They close their eyes and cover their faces. Coming upon the bar, they notice the broken window is now covered with a huge piece of plywood. In black spray paint appears "Fags go home." Under this, in small letters, someone has written, "This is our home."

Entering the bar, they see Maybellene playing pool with a man.

"Who is that?" Emma wonders.

"Uch!" Robin recognizes him at once. "Some repulsive straight man who comes in here. Barnaby says we shouldn't even look at him."

"I'm sure Maybellene can handle him." They notice Barnaby perched like a spaced-out stork on his favorite barstool. They approach him cautiously.

"Don't despair," Emma begins, "it won't last much longer."

He smiles weakly. "I have become a man-hating faggot. How can there be such a thing?" He stares morosely into his drink. "I thought it would surely pass, but it is getting worse. My life is about to be ruined by a contradiction."

Robin immediately feels useful, like Freud at a convention of neurotics. He found himself in this same absurd position three years ago. He whispers to Barnaby, "Faggots are not really men."

Barnaby starts and then snorts. "How do you explain that thing between their legs, then?"

"Don't get bogged down in biology. They once called us the third sex, remember? They were right. We've come here to show men how they can love each other, give each other pleasure, and make each other happy."

70

Barnaby sits up, reaches his long arm around Robin's neck, pulls him suddenly and forcefully to him and kisses him for a full minute before letting go.

"That's it." Robin has a hard-on. Rosa and Emma applaud.

"We had to come above ground. The men are too far gone. Somebody had to do something."

"They've always been gone," Barnaby states.

"Of course. And when they only had clubs and guns we could be discrete, stay out of sight and watch. People had a chance to survive then. Now they have B-52's and atom bombs and poisons. You can't let people as crazed as they are have such deadly things to play with." Robin is warming up. "I went to the baths. There were five hundred fags there, naked and horny and stoned. And there was not even a hint of violence."

"Plenty of competition," Barnaby snaps.

"Sure. But in all the years, and honey, I am talking about *years*, I have been going to the baths I have never seen a single fight. That's amazing. Straight men never have that experience with other men. Never."

"Het men, ugh!" Emma copes by pretending that het men, as she calls them, do not exist. It has proven easier than she imagined. She has none for friends. She only works with them when she is forced to and she ignores them on the street whenever possible. They are like a rash which might go away if you don't scratch it too much.

Robin is feeling carried away. Barnaby hands him a drink and a joint. "By 1969 we realized that we were still sane in spite of having been forced to hide out in those wretched closets for so long. The men had become so greedy and violent that we figured we'd better surface to show them some other way to be. We could no longer hide in our closets playing with each other. We had to go public."

"Do you think it has worked?" Emma asks with a smirk.

"It doesn't seem to have helped that much. But we are trying." Robin retreats a bit to think over his position. Emma plunges ahead.

"If het men, a subject I dislike discussing, you understand, but if het men had to clean out their own toilets and bathtubs and wash their own floors and clothes, they would not make so many messes. Anyone who has ever washed dishes every day for a few years would think twice before creating a chemical dump that has to be cleaned up someday. Het men are now making messes that cannot even be cleaned up. They make nuclear waste dumps, knowing that they do not know how to clean them up. No rational animal shits in its own refrigerator."

Robin is inspired by Emma's wisdom. "So we are here to stop het men from destroying it all. We only look like men. We are really something else. You should never think that when you make love to a faggot you are making love to a man."

"What about all those butch faggots in the West Village?"

"It's all attitude and drag."

"We're all such sweet transvestites . . ." Rosa sings, smiling.

"That's close."

Suddenly they hear Maybellene screaming, "I told you that's against the rules." Her partner, the straight man, stares at her. "You don't cheat on Maybellene Donit, honey." He does not move. "Did you hear me?" He acts like he does not. "What are you doing in here anyway? We don't like straight guys in our bar. Now get out." She grabs his pool cue out of his hand. "I said good-bye." He turns around and walks slowly to the door. Maybellene is right behind him, pointing her pool cue at his back.

At the door he turns his head slightly and says, "You'll get yours, you dumb dyke."

"I've already got mine, buster," she replies, but he is gone. "He thought he could pull a fast one on me," she explains to the sound of scattered applause. "Who's ready for a game of pool?" she asks, moving quickly back to the table.

"I told you Maybellene could handle him."

"I feel so much better." Barnaby flashes a smile.

"What if he goes out and organizes all his straight men

friends?" Emma feels slightly apprehensive.

"They are already organized."

"Don't worry." Robin strokes Emma's arm. "Straight men don't have friends. They have business associates and drinking buddies. But hardly ever friends. I once had my class write a paper about friendship. The women talked on and on about this one and that one and how they couldn't live without them. The men were pitiful. A few had had a friend in high school whom they remembered fondly but whom they hadn't seen in years; a couple others had an army buddy they once felt close to as they suffered through basic training together; one had his brother. But not much else. It's sad, really."

"I couldn't live without my friends," Rosa exclaims. "Who would console you after a ruined romance? Who would you dish with?"

"Straight men don't dish, they brag." Barnaby pauses to take a drink of white wine. "Didn't you learn as a kid that gossip is frivolous, something only silly women do over coffee because they don't have anything important to think about?"

"I'd die without my daily dose of gossip."

"That's why you're a faggot, Rosa."

Emma is concentrating. "I realize I am nervous about falling in love because I'm afraid I won't have time for my friends. Maybe that's a little extreme."

"But if you get everything you need from your friends, why bother with love? I think you are smart. That's why I'm off romance. Lovers take too much time and give too little back."

"I get most things I need. But I could use a little more sex."

"I have a boyfriend, yet I have all my sex with strangers. The categories don't make much sense to me anymore." Robin is confused.

"You cannot be said to be having a love affair with another person if you do not have sex with him, seldom see him, and when you do, seldom talk." Rosa is definite. "Robin, there is no mystery here at all." Robin looks so sad that Rosa becomes concerned. "How do you feel about it?" he asks, turning "feel" into a five-syllable word.

"Angry and then not angry. Secure."

"Secure?" Rosa screams incredulously.

"Charlie comes home every night. At some point."

"But not always alone."

"Only once did he..."

"Once is once too often." Rosa feels the last word has been spoken.

"This whole thing is dog meat." Robin is on the verge of feeling sorry for himself.

"Dog meat beats no meat," Emma quips, wondering if she might not be ready to fall in love after all.

Rosa puts an arm around Robin's shoulder and gives him a squeeze. Gently, he says, "You are holding on to nothing."

"You can't hold on to nothing," Robin states firmly.

"Honey, maybe not, but you are clutching the void harder than any queen I know."

Robin is slightly desperate. "It was something nice once."

"So was the Love Canal, I hear."

"It's a new kind of relationship, one without possessiveness."

"Or sex, or contact, or talk."

Robin is now quite undone. All Rosa's words sound right but they barely register with his emotions. Some mystery has overtaken him. The language, though he understands it, does not mean anything to his emotions. 'It must be a contradiction that I don't understand yet. My life is full; the world is heading towards its end; I know that I no longer have a boyfriend, yet it feels like I still have a boyfriend. We are still living together. That must mean something.'

He is stirred out of his morose wonderings by a poke in his rib. He looks up in time to see a woman slide past him. She moves so quickly to a dark corner that he catches only the color of her hair—white and pink.

"That's her," Emma's eyes announce.

"I can't see her," Rosa complains.

"Don't stare. Be cool," Emma hisses. Maybellene leaves in the middle of the pool game among loud complaints, to join the woman in the corner.

Emma pats down her black hair, straightens her shirt and lights a joint. "If you boys will excuse me, mamma has some subtle sleuthing to do. I intend to be introduced. Who knows, she might have a friend." Emma feels hot at the thought of it. She walks casually across the room, kicking cigarette butts, stopping to inspect each old hubcap as she passes, glancing upwards as if she had just spotted a flock of wild geese and finally disappears into the dark corner.

"Subtlety was never her strong point." They turn back to the bar for some serious drinking.

9

A BREEDER IN THEIR MIDST

The heat is off. It is forty degrees outside and forty degrees inside. Robin is wearing long underwear, sweat pants, a T-shirt, a flannel shirt, a sweat shirt and a sweater. He feels a bit overproduced.

A strong wind rattles the windows. Sirens wail and horns blare on Second Avenue. Robin ambles to the window. A city bus sits in the middle of the street, looking abandoned, jamming traffic. A screaming ambulance is caught in the tie-up. Robin walks back to the sofa and slumps on it.

'The ruling class has abandoned America,' he thinks. 'They have squeezed all they can out of us. There are more profits to be made in Taiwan and Brazil, so all the money we made for them is now sent elsewhere. The abandoned bus and the stalled ambulance wailing outside make my present situation perfectly clear. It is collapsing around me. But why doesn't anything ever happen to David Rockefeller? His planes never crash, his office never catches fire, he is never shot at, mugged or beaten up. He never gets food poisoning, falls off a tall building or drowns. I hear he even walks to work and he never falls in a pot hole, steps in dog shit or gets hassled for spare change. No one breaks into his house; no one spits in his face; no one knifes him. His tranquillity is only disturbed by small cracks in his empire. He doesn't live that far away from me, but he sure lives in a different world than I do.'

He begins to revive the Kissinger kidnap fantasy when the phone rings.

"This is Bruce."

"I'm freezing to death."

"I'm losing energy."

77

"Get real, Bruce."

"I'm losing energy, I tell you. When I get up in the morning my body barely responds to my mind. It moves about sluggishly. I drink cod-liver oil, take my vitamins and even exercise. What do they want from me?"

"Did you go to the doctor?" Robin asks without thinking.

"Of course not," snaps Bruce. "I am losing energy. What the hell do doctors know about that?"

"Maybe you've been to too many rock 'n' roll clubs."

"Rock 'n' roll gives me energy."

"Maybe everyone else is using too much. They are stealing some of yours. Maybe there are too many people for the amount of energy around."

"Do you feel it, Robin?"

"I might. But I've been taking so many drugs it's hard to tell."

"Oh, yeah? Anything good?"

"Nothing to help you."

"I decided if I stayed home, then I could protect my energy. But it doesn't seem to help. I need an hour of sleep for every hour I'm awake. Maybe the Lower East Side is wiping me out."

"Maybe it's your new boyfriend. Romance can take a lot out of you."

"I could give Barnaby more. But he doesn't want more. He keeps wanting less."

"Maybe less is more," suggests Robin.

"It seems so pointless. I do not have the energy to wash the dishes and clean up the bathroom. I can only do one. I try to decide which one to do and realize that neither is worth doing. They are both pointless when it is all winding down. There are too many evil people putting out too much evil energy and building hideous bombs and chemicals and fighting and ugh! who needs it. Maybe people are fading off the scene. A blessing if you ask me."

"So you're part of the cosmic fade-out," Robin says reassuringly.

"But it puts me in a rotten mood." He is quiet for a moment. "I'm too tired to talk anymore."

"I'm too cold."

"You can come over here and get warm if you want."

"No. It's good to suffer some. I'll just sit here and think about the bombing of Leningrad."

"What about a Siberian labor camp?"

"Soon."

"Soon."

They both kiss the telephone and hang up. Before he can reach the sofa, the phone rings again.

Rosa is screaming, "Run to the window. There are two drag queens walking down Second Avenue. Real live drag queens. Bye. Got to call the others."

Robin flies to the window, moves some plants, opens it and climbs out onto the fire escape. He spots them at once. They are out for a public stroll, dressed for high tea with Jackie O. at the Plaza, giving smiles and delicate waves to the astonished street people.

"Yoo-hoo," Robin shouts down at them. When they look up he gives them a limp wrist and a wink. They wave their handkerchiefs demurely. The ambulance is gone but the abandoned bus continues to slow traffic. Drivers, noticing the show, honk. Robin claps his hands with delight. 'Drag queens can still stop traffic. Maybe all is not lost,' he thinks cheerily. He blows them a kiss as they pass on down the street.

Shivering, he comes back in but before he can reach the sofa the buzzer rings. He walks down the long hall and presses the button. He opens the door and screams down the stairwell, "Who's there?"

Barnaby strolls in. "Let's get going."

"Where?" Robin feebly asks as he settles on the sofa in between Auden and Gloria, who are snoozing.

"Where? We have to hand out these leaflets if we want anyone to come to the demonstration."

"No one will come anyway."

"Let's not be cynical. Remember the sixties."

"That's when everyone had long hair and marched around a lot, wasn't it?"

"That's when people were hopeful and political."

"Ah, come on," Robin moans, "let's just sit here and keep warm and talk about Chile and torture and ITT."

"Robin, don't force me into guilt-tripping you."

Robin is adamant. "I will not hand out flyers to people who don't want them, won't read them and throw them on the street. They either ignore you or laugh at you or, if they happen to glance at the flyer, sneer at you. It is masochistic. I will not subject myself to public humiliation."

"What about a little private humiliation then?" Barnaby winks.

"That's different. What I do in the privacy of my own bedroom..."

"O.K., O.K." Barnaby feels impatient and frustrated. "What do you suggest?"

"Let's call our friends and alert them."

"I did that. All nine of them."

Robin snuggles deeper into the lavender sofa, pulling Auden up around his neck like a feather boa. Auden lets out a screech and flings himself off Robin.

Barnaby is pacing the floor trying to become agitated. He thinks of high-strung Russian nihilists and intense Spanish anarchists, trying to work himself into decisiveness. He paces faster. Suddenly he turns on Robin and shouts, "We must do something."

Robin sighs. Apathy in the face of fanaticism is useless. "Let's put them up on the buildings. I have all of Charlie's stuff from the night he was beat up putting up posters," he adds, thinking this might temper Barnaby's enthusiasm.

"Great, let's go."

They walk out of the building into a swirling cloud of dirt that is making its way slowly down the street. They step back into the doorway to let it pass. It is followed by two complete copies of the *Daily News* and three empty beer cans. When the garbage subsides they begin doing the street. Robin pours Carnation evaporated milk into a pail, dips a paint brush in and paints the flyers that Barnaby holds on the wall. Cold evaporated milk slides down Barnaby's fingers and hands.

"Saw two real live drag queens right on this street this afternoon. The first I've seen in months."

"Amazing. Where have they all gone anyway? Do you know?"

"They all moved to Houston and Dallas and Atlanta, I hear."

"For the climate?"

"No, 'cause that's where the men are still men and the women are still women. It is impossible to be a drag queen in a place where are there no real machos left."

"I want to sleep with one."

"With their clothes off they look just like we do."

Barnaby's hands have become stiff with freezing evaporated milk. He can barely pick up the flyers.

"Is this unpleasant enough for you?" Robin asks.

Barnaby sneers, "It's so unpleasant it almost seems important."

In silence, relishing their sacrifice, they continue for two more blocks, which puts them in front of the bar. They cover the plywood window with their flyers.

"Leave that showing," Robin commands, pointing to "How can we destroy and kill ourselves while our killers stand alive and waiting." Reading it they feel that it was put there especially for their benefit.

Before they reach the nearly deserted bar, Emma is at their side. Robin thrusts the rest of the leaflets into her hands. She looks at them and barks, "Oh, I know, I know."

"Are you coming?" Robin thinks he sounds nearly threatening.

"Of course, of course." Emma often talks double when she is excited. "But this is nothing. I've got dish, deep, deep dish."

"That's better than a drink," Robin says.

"Scarlet has missed her period, definitely missed it." Robin and Barnaby look at each other and sigh. "Well, you know what that means."

"It's abortion time in ole New York," Robin says sadly.

"No, no." Emma is warming up the dish. "No, no."

"What do you mean 'No, no'?"

"Just that." She smiles triumphantly, her red lips parting and her black mascaraed eyes flashing. The two collapse on barstools and order white wine.

Barnaby turns to Emma, who is still transfixed by her coup, to ask, "Who's she been fucking?"

"Some artist."

"Black?"

"Well, of course. Who else would she fuck?"

"Her Jewish mother in Brooklyn will be thrilled."

"She can't have a baby," Robin says emphatically.

"Watch her," Emma replies defiantly as if she is the one who is having the kid.

"She sells dope, shoots coke and spends every night in rock 'n' roll clubs."

"She says she'll clean up her act."

"What about this black artist? Is he ready for cuddly-coos and smelly diapers?"

"She does not plan to involve him at all. It is, after all, none of his business." Emma's speech is becoming more restrained and clipped as she realizes she is about to be forced to defend motherhood, a state she has always considered the pits. "She is thirty-five. It is now or never and I am entirely confident that she can handle it all."

"Fucking breeders," Barnaby snarls and turns away to face the bar. He focuses his mind on the storming of the Winter Palace.

"Breeding is out, Emma. There are too many people already. What can she be thinking of?"

"She wants a kid."

82

"But why? Motherhood is slavery."

"Only the first few years."

"How many years?"

"Well, I don't know. Ten, maybe."

"Or fifteen?"

"O.K. So what? It's not your life."

"Nobody with any sense brings a kid into this world. It'll be twenty-one in the year 2000. Even the federal government says this place will be uninhabitable by 2000. For its twenty-first birthday we'll give it a dead planet. Breeders are idiots." Robin turns his back on Emma. Emma sighs, realizing that only last week she delivered the exact same speech to Robin when Robin informed her that three of his students were pregnant. She steps to the bar and orders a double scotch on the rocks, pulls out a joint, lights it and passes it along the bar.

One deep inhale of dope and Robin is lost in images of babies born with stumps for legs, with no mouth openings, with elongated heads. "I read they just found out that another of those insecticides they spray all over forests causes miscarriages and deformed babies. Doesn't she read the papers?"

After the soldiers have shot the people down in front of the Winter Palace, Barnaby's mind fades back to the bar. "How is she going to support it?"

"Mothers can be dope dealers, you know," Emma answers. "That is the least of it."

"Does she think Love Canal is only in Buffalo?"

"She'll eat organic."

"And stop breathing, I suppose."

"She'll leave the city."

"She might as well. She's already left her mind someplace."

Robin is beginning to feel very sad. "Scarlet was such a nice sensible woman. Now she's joining the breeders. It's too frightening."

"It's not like she's been born again or joined the CIA," Emma replies.

"It changes people. Breeders all feel superior to us nonbreeders. They feel sorry for us. Isn't that the question they always ask us queers? 'How do you feel about not having any children?' They are slaves to their children who then grow up to hate them. They can't stand us for escaping all that. She'll end up like the rest, hating us for our freedom and feeling superior for having done the noble deed of carrying on the species. Sometimes I think that's why homosexuals are so hated. We are too smart to get trapped by biology."

"If there aren't any kids, the old men can't fight wars. Hitler paid women to have kids."

"Well, she's not going to have a boy anyway. She's having a girl."

"What?" Robin is incredulous.

"She figured it out."

"And what if her scheme fails and a boy pops out?"

"She'll give it away to some faggot who wants to raise a boy."

"Give it away?"

"Well, you can't expect a dyke feminist to raise a boy child now, can you?"

"I don't know what a dyke feminist is doing fucking men in the first place."

"Well, he is black."

"I'm going home before I throw up."

"Robin, I know how you feel, but I was thinking..."

"Emma. No."

"Well, I am thirty-six and it might be nice to have a little..."

"Emma, go home, take a Quaalude, sleep it off. It will pass, I'm sure it will pass."

"I was just thinking..."

"Don't think. Have another double scotch on me." He orders the drink and takes her hands and kisses them several times. "We are enough of a family, Emma. You don't need any more. Believe me."

"I know. But if I got some people to be co-parents we could, like, do it communally, you know, like a group, communally." She flashes a weak smile and slugs down her drink.

"Emma," Robin starts very patiently, "remember Bernadette Dorhan, the stray dog we all adopted. 'With so many of us, she won't be a burden to anyone,' we said. And now she's Leslie's dog and Leslie lives in Vancouver alone with the dog. And remember Sadie our VW bus, Sadie who sat on East Fourth Street for two weeks with a flat tire 'cause we were all too busy to cope and by the time we remembered to do something, there was nothing left but the steering wheel. Emma, be real."

The scotch did it. Emma smiles. "We'll see. I'd have to get pregnant first and that, in itself, would be a major production."

"I'm sure Ruby would help you out," Robin says, remembering the three times Emma and Ruby had made it together.

"Oh, he doesn't like to fuck. You know that. He only plays around like some little kid."

"But you don't like to get fucked either," Robin reminds her.

"I know. That's why Ruby is so great to do it with." Sex talk always makes Emma excited, any kind of sex talk, any time. "Who else? I saw a gorgeous Asian man in the deli yesterday. Or maybe Rosa could be enticed. He always says he'd like to see what fucking a woman is like. Maybe. But I guess the smartest thing would be artificial insemination. I'll get some good specimen to jack off..."

"In front of you, no doubt."

"Naturally and then I'll just squirt it in."

"Emma, stop talking dirty."

"But I'm getting off."

"I realize."

Trying to find a way back to reality, Barnaby asks, "How are you going to support this kid?"

"I'll become a hooker."

"Who doesn't like to get fucked?"

"I'll be a novelty act."

They all nearly smile.

"I must talk with Scarlet," Robin says firmly.

"She does not want to be harassed. She needs support right now."

"I won't hassle her. I just want to point out a few things."

"They have all been pointed out to her." She quickly puts on her coat. "I can think of at least four people who have not heard the news yet, and I must be the first to tell them. Ta, ta." And she is out the door.

Barnaby stares into his drink. "Breeders. They're pitiful," he says softly.

"What?"

"Breeding. What a stink hole. Parents and children devour each other. If it isn't one way it's another. You know, Robin," turning earnest, "I've always considered my homosexuality to be a form of patricide. I came out to my straight brother first. He remained quite calm but said emphatically not to tell our parents under any circumstances. He said right out, 'It would kill Dad.' When I told Mom, she said she'd known for a long time, maybe because that was what she'd been hoping for. But she repeated the threat. 'Your father would die if he knew,' she said to me."

"So naturally you told your father."

"Naturally," Barnaby replies with a shrug. "And when I did I knew I had diminished, if only by a little, the power of men in this world. My father felt betrayed. Betrayed! I was surprised he saw it so clearly. Because being a faggot is a form of betrayal. It's one of the few kinds of betrayal they still take seriously. When I became a faggot it was clear to me that I was walking out on my responsibility to the patriarchy. I would not take a woman and subject her to my will. I would not have kids and teach them, by example, that men are on top. I would not plot with other men to rule the planet." He is quiet for a moment. "My father would have killed me if the law and my mother had

86

not stood in his way."

"Fathers are always looking for reasons to kill their sons. If they can do it, it cuts the competition. It is, after all, old men who send young men off to die in wars which the old men start and run." Robin has not seen this so clearly before. It is a new idea and new ideas excite him. He is forced to order another white wine to calm down.

"The old men of Britain managed to wipe out an entire generation of young men in World War I. That must have made them feel secure."

"Men hold on to power until they drop dead. Look at the Senate or China. And to hold on they have to keep all those young men at bay." Robin suddenly is jolted nearly off his seat by Rosa's body lunging into him.

"I thought I'd find you degenerates here. I have news that's too hot."

"Oh?" Barnaby says, looking totally disinterested.

"Did you see the drag queens?" he asks. Robin nods. "Well, I followed them and talked to them and they invited me to a party." Robin and Barnaby look at him blankly. "Tonight," Rosa exclaims, trying to generate some excitement. "One of them is Puerto Rican and one, you'll never believe this, is Italian. Who ever heard of an Italian drag queen? So come on."

'Maybe I can get laid,' Barnaby thinks as Rosa moves them out of the bar. Robin carries the pail of evaporated milk and Barnaby carries the paint brush. After a half-hour search of Second Street they realize Rosa was given an imaginary address.

"God, if you can't trust drag queens, who can you trust?"

10

THE POOR PLOT

Robin is surprised when he wakes up with a hangover. He moans in bed for a while wondering if Charlie has gone to work or not. Charlie is erratic about when he will allow his boss the pleasure of his company. If he is angry at some injustice or, more likely, bored with the work, he simply does not show up for several days.

Charlie bounces into the room with a hot cup of tea. "Caffeine for my sleepy boy."

"You're so good to me," Robin mumbles, feeling guilty about staying out late again, getting smashed, and then waking Charlie up as he banged around the apartment trying to maneuver himself into bed. 'If only I didn't remember it all these days. Blackouts were quite useful, like being psychotic for an evening. You don't have to be responsible for yourself for a while.' Robin resolves to stop feeling guilty.

Charlie scurries around the bedroom hanging up clothes. "I'm going upstairs to feed Phoebe's dog before work."

"Is she away?"

"She and her new girlfriend went to Atlantic City for a few days."

"In March?"

"It's cheaper this time of year."

"I bet."

"Maybe I'll have sex with Jose." Charlie drops the remark casually. Robin pretends he hasn't heard anything. "After I fed him yesterday I sat on the couch with my pants down and while I was playing with myself he started licking my ass, but I was uptight so I made him stop. But I've been thinking about it ever since." Charlie says all this as quickly as possible.

"Oh, my nerves." Robin grabs Auden, who is sprawled out on the bed pretending to sleep, and sticks him under the covers. Auden yells and scrambles out.

"Do you want to come watch?" Charlie asks in his sweetest voice.

Robin has to think. 'It is the first sex offer I've gotten from Charlie in many months and one thing could lead to another, but, no, I have some pride.' "It's too early. I'm too hung over. Dogs don't turn me on. Besides, what's in it for me?" Robin slowly sinks under the covers hoping Charlie will tell him what's in it for him. 'I don't have that much pride.'

"O.K. See you soon," and Charlie is out the door.

Robin had planned to spend the morning thinking about peasant poverty and Coca-Cola profits in Guatemala and the CIA plots that keep it going but he knows he is now condemned to think about Charlie's asshole and Jose's tongue. When the phone rings he climbs out of bed, steps on Gloria's tail and hobbles to answer it.

"Maybellene here. How are you sweets?"

"You sound alive and well and living in Argentina."

"My crush is devouring me."

"I haven't met her yet," Robin says, trying to be pointed.

"I'm pretending it's low-keyed by not introducing her to any of my friends if I can help it, though Emma managed to worm an introduction out of me last night."

"What's her name? At least you can give out that." Robin starts a slow probe.

"Flow."

"As in Flo she don't know but the boy she loves is Romeo?"

"As in river."

"Naturally. And what's her story?"

"She's been everywhere, done everything. Any place where there have ever been at least two dykes, she has been. Plays the piano and you know what a music lover I am. She is intense, I admit. Emma said she is psychotic but you know how petty people are around here. If you're the least bit weird, you're psychotic. I'd say more that she's desperate."

"For what?"

"Me, I hope."

"I suppose you've heard about Scarlet."

"That girl is too gone. Her brain has wilted. I'm having drinks with her today. Don't worry, I'll bounce her back to reality. Oh, no, there's Flow in her window, waving to me, naked. Got to go. Kisses." And she is gone.

Robin reaches for an old *New York Times* lying on the floor and sighs. 'Am I upset that Charlie is having sex with a dog upstairs? Am I losing my boyfriend to a dog, not even a cute lovable dog but a mean mutt? I didn't say a word about Charlie and Ruby in the toilet,' he thinks. 'Maybe that was a mistake. If a relationship is to prosper someone has to be willing to suffer sometimes. Someone has to be willing to get hurt when the other person breaks a rule. But is there a rule against dogs? I doubt it.'

Finding it all too baroque, he glances at the *Times*, the newspaper of government handouts, until he notices a story about 10,000 birds dead in Newburgh, New York, from eating poisoned fertilizer. They were found by a farmer one morning, hanging from trees and lying on bushes and hedges. 'Perfect,' he thinks, 'I must tell this one to Scarlet.'

While Robin is thinking about dead birds, Charlie roars into the apartment. "It was great. You shoulda been there. He licked my ass and then when I came he licked up all the cum." He squeals to indicate happiness.

"Great," Robin mumbles as he tries to focus his mind on Guatemala, but the dead birds won't go away.

"I'm going to work."

"It's before noon."

"I know, but Mr. Monster won't be there today so I can get all caught up on my work without Fire Throat breathing down my neck. And then to the theater. Do you work today?"

"Yeah."

"So I'll see you later. You'll be at the Terminal, I take it," a hint of disapproval in his voice.

"I may stay in tonight."

"Planning to break your leg?"

"It would be easier than breaking your heart."

"It was only a dog."

"Go to work." Charlie bends down and kisses Robin on the head and flies out the door.

Haunted by dead birds, Robin dresses and starts for school. He buys a current *Times*, hoping for more news about the birds. '10,000 is so many,' he thinks, entering the subway. There is a pronounced smoky smell but no evidence of smoke. He goes through the turnstile just as the train pulls in. He settles in a seat and opens the paper. After two stops the train comes to a screeching halt in between two stations and begins to fill up with smoke, slowly.

Everyone in his car looks scared, except for an old toothless man sitting across from him who yells out, "It happens all the time. No bother. No bother," and begins rocking back and forth. He does not reassure Robin.

An official enters the car. "There's a fire ahead. Please move to the back of the train. There's no danger." A woman begins to scream at him in Spanish. All the passengers walk car after car until everyone is crowded into the last two cars. Smoke follows them.

Suddenly the doors open and they are helped out of the car onto the tracks where thick black smoke swirls everywhere. They walk a short distance, covering their faces, yet still coughing, to the station they just passed. They climb up onto the platform and are told to leave at once. 'Don't I even get a refund?' Robin thinks, but he says nothing. On the street he walks a few blocks until he finds a cab.

On the ferry ride he feels shaky and smells smoky.

He arrives too late for his first class. He had decided to talk about nuclear annihilation. 'It's probably just as well I missed it. I might have gotten really depressed,' he thinks.

The second class is about half empty. 'People can't even get to school anymore.' He tells the class about the fire. "The random collapse of the infrastructure suits their purposes well," he begins. "It keeps us all scared, off balance and off the streets. They like us to be isolated, in our separate apartments and fearful. Rape serves the same purpose. It is a form of terrorism practiced by men against women. Random violence is the most effective terrorist tactic there is. If it's random, then it is not connected to anything you do but to who you are. You get raped not because you are bad, not because you did anything wrong, but simply because you are a woman." 'Or a faggot,' he thinks but does not say it. "The U.S. Air Force used to bomb Vietnamese villages at random to try to create terror in order to elicit submission to their will by the peasants. Rapists are the men's goon squads out there showing women their place."

By the end of the class Robin is overwrought, the women are depressed and the men wish they hadn't come. He leaves school immediately.

The bus up First Avenue is empty. It rattles slowly along the street. He looks through the *Times* for diversion. He reads about the discovery of an old radium dump in Colorado left over from the radium industry that collapsed in the twenties. He remembers that women would lick their brushes to make them stiff, dip them in radium and then paint watch faces so they would glow in the dark. Most of the women died of tongue cancer. This is the twenty-first contaminated dump found so far in the state of Colorado. Utah, he learns, still has high levels of plutonium left over from the A-bomb tests in the fifties. The 10,000 dead birds return to his mind. 'What must the farmer have thought when he woke to find them all there?' A nuclear power plant is shut down in Oswego, New York, on the shores of Lake Ontario because it cannot withstand an earthquake. Engrossed in this news from the apocalypse, he rides far beyond his stop. When he notices, he leaps up and gets off. He is in front of a movie theater. *Norma Rae* is playing. 'I'll go,' he thinks. 'A movie about a union victory. I could definitely use

93

that.' The ticket seller tells him it is sold out. 'A union movie sold out. What can that mean?' He walks downtown. He passes someone who reminds him in some way he can't define of Harvey Milk, the first and maybe the last left gay politician in America assassinated by a storm trooper. He passes a gay pornographic theater. 'I'll suck one for Harvey,' he thinks.

The theater is small. Downstairs, where he goes with only a glance at the film, is very dark. A few steps into the room brings him in contact with two men having sex who, with their hands, invite him to join them. They are both gentle with him, rubbing his body and playing with his cock. He drops his pants. One of them caresses his cock with his mouth. He kisses the other man. Then they take turns kissing and sucking. One by one they each have an orgasm held tightly by the other two.

They thank each other for such a nice time and leave the dark basement one at a time. Robin watches part of a movie to collect himself. Leaving, he sends a kiss to Harvey.

He walks towards the bar. At Sixth Street he sees the limousines again. Only two of them this time. Long, sleek and black. He walks casually by them, peering in out of the corner of his eye. Each has a black driver wearing a uniform but no passengers. 'They have something to do with the dead birds and Guatemala and Kissinger. That much I'm sure of.' Feeling slightly off balance by the sight, he hurries to the bar.

'Is this bar closed?' he thinks, walking in. He sees no one. He rouses the bartender, who is engrossed in looking through a dirty magazine, and orders a white wine.

Then out of the darkness of the far corner he hears an unmistakable shriek, "Fired. Me. The hottest busboy in New York." It is Rosa in hysterics.

"You were too hot, I guess."

"I didn't even steal much from those lowlife hets. Some silverware, a little money and one, just one, silver creamer which turned another color just yesterday. I worked my ass off and they fire me." Robin walks the full length of the bar where Rosa is fuming to Ruby. "Did you hear?"

"My hearing aid was turned up all the way. What happened, hon?" He puts his arm around Rosa's shoulder and gives him a hug.

"They fired me. Said I was too flamboyant. They were worried I'd offend the customers."

"But all the customers are queer."

"Discreetly queer. The place is in Soho, remember? It's all right to be queer these days as long as you're bourgeois about it. Fired me. They paid me dog shit, drained me to total exhaustion and made me work off the books so now there's no unemployment money. I'll have to find another job or starve. Get this queen out of this town. It's just too much." Rosa becomes limp.

Ruby smells a chance. "We'll rip them off. We'll go there some night and steal the money. It'll be your unemployment insurance."

"I'm too scared."

"They must keep the money there overnight."

"Yeah, they do."

"How much?" Ruby feels he is about to score.

"Depends."

"Five thou?"

"At least."

"Where?"

"In the basement. In a safe."

"Is the safe locked?"

"Not usually."

"Is there a window in the back?"

"Yeah. Into the kitchen."

"Perfect." Ruby is ready. "We'll split it. Fifty-fifty."

"What if we get caught?"

"We won't. We'll plan it all out." The idea penetrates Rosa's histrionics and he straightens himself up to think more clearly about it.

"They are scum, het scum. They barely paid me the minimum wage, which is more than they pay the illegal

Mexicans who do all the cooking. You can't live on that. One of the gay waiters told me he heard one of the managers call the customers 'a bunch of queers.' Can you imagine insulting the people who support you?"

"Rosa, it's part of a chain. The managers probably don't even own it. They probably just work there," Robin says, trying to undermine this folly.

"All the better. We'll be stealing from some big corporation. They steal enough from us." Ruby's point shuts Robin up.

Ruby notices he has a hard-on. He immediately pokes Robin with it.

"You'll have an orgasm in the safe." Robin squeezes his cock.

"This is just what I need to turn my head around."

"Is something wrong?"

"I think I'm depressed."

"Depressed? Why?"

"You can ask? Spring isn't here. I don't have a job. The draft is coming back, which always means war. Love Canal is just the first and political prisoners are being tortured all over the world."

"I'm sorry I asked."

"How do you know you're depressed?" Rosa is curious about the symptoms.

"All I want to do is have anonymous sex and get drunk. I even went to the baths. You know me. I only have sex with someone after I have spent six months flirting with him."

"Or her," Robin reminds him.

Ruby frowns. "But I need contact with anyone, everyone. I want to lie down on the sidewalk with half the people I see on the street and make love to them. But I can't, so I drink. I think it means I'm depressed. A good robbery is just what I need to bring me right up."

Robin undoes the top button of Ruby's jeans and slips his hand down the front of his pants.

"Maybe you two should retire to the toilet."

"I'm just consoling this poor delicate queen."

Bruce is suddenly at their side. "I could use some consoling too," he says, ordering a drink.

"Me too, me too." Rosa is feverish. "Bruce, I was fired."

"From Beer, Burgers and Beef Stew?"

"The same. For being too swishy. I never even knew you could be too swishy. Oh," he groans, "their children should all turn queer."

"But we're going to get their asses," Ruby says in his most menacing voice. His cock twitches. Ruby pulls Bruce close to him and lowers his voice. "We are going to rip them off. Want to join us? We could use a good lookout."

"You mean steal?"

"We think of it as redistributing a little of the wealth," Rosa says. "I'm only taking what is due me."

"How much?"

"We can't be sure. Maybe a couple of grand apiece."

Robin notices that they have each begun to adopt a new voice and a new accent. They all sound vaguely like Jimmy Cagney. It makes him think that they might just be serious. His mind struggles to find objections. Finally he says as seriously as possible, "If you get caught . . ."

"Don't even think of such a thing. You'll bad vibe the whole operation," Rosa says cheerfully, patting Robin's cheek. "Tomorrow I have to go in and pick up my check, my last check. I'll have a good look around. Then tomorrow night, they close at two, we can case the joint."

Robin removes his hand from Ruby's pants. He glumly orders another white wine.

Ruby sways with excitement. "It's perfect. It's clean. Correct. You know I feel like Robin Hood. Maybe I'll wear a feather."

"What about running shoes and a gun?" Robin says nervously.

"Guns?" Rosa will have none of it. "Clever crooks do not need weapons. It's only those big, greedy, clumsy ones like

Chase Manhattan and ITT who need to use weapons to get their way. We have our wits." Robin looks at him astonished. "Well, sometimes I have my wits." He winks at Robin. "Now let's not bring up all those nights when I was giving too much gone." He suddenly swirls on his barstool and shrieks, "Oh, Barn, hon," to the door where Barnaby stands, glowering.

Suddenly Bruce gathers up his things. "Tomorrow, then." He kisses Rosa on the cheek and Robin on the mouth.

Robin mutters, "Be careful," but Bruce is gone.

Barnaby approaches them, bristling with attitude.

"Hi, sweets," Robin says coyly. "How are you doing?"

"Fine." Barnaby's tone indicates clearly that that is all the information anyone is about to get. Rosa and Robin pretend to be entranced by the Talking Heads singing. "This ain't no party, this ain't no disco, this ain't no fooling around. This ain't no Mudd Club, no CBGB. I ain't got no time for that now." Robin sings to the music, waving his head back and forth. Rosa checks out his nails. Barnaby puts a white pill in his mouth, washes it down with a gulp of bourbon and frowns. "Romance is nauseating."

"When it's over, it's over."

"It's over?"

"Over."

Rosa, catching the drift, exclaims, "With you and Bruce? But just two nights ago you were smooching it up over there by the pool table."

"Two nights? What do two nights mean?"

Rosa is stumped. 'What do two nights mean anyway? I could be dead two nights from now or two nights ago.' The thought of death always makes every human concept or activity seem meaningless to Rosa.

"Does Bruce know it's over?" Robin asks cautiously.

"I doubt it." Abruptly, Barnaby picks up his drink and strides to the other side of the bar. Rosa and Robin give each other a "pardon me" look.

"You will walk me home, won't you?" Rosa asks, putting

himself together.

"Only if you let me talk you out of this foolishness."

"Oh, darling. Don't be humdrum. Life is too sad, too dull to miss such an opportunity for excitement, not to mention the money. And it's so clean."

11

WE ARE ALL BUMS IN AMERICA

The phone rings all morning.

First it is Rosa. "It's twenty degrees outside. You can't have a demonstration in the winter."

"Wear long underwear," Robin advises.

Then it is Bruce. "Do you think Barnaby is still angry with me?"

"He didn't seem that friendly last night." 'I guess he doesn't know yet,' thinks Robin sadly.

"Oh, we had this tiff. Nothing really, or I hope it's nothing. I said that I thought demonstrations were liberal and he said that excessive criticism of political actions was reactionary and . . ."

"Come to the demonstration. Show him how much you care for him by doing something liberal." Robin smiles to himself, pleased with how well he can manage his friends' sordid affairs.

Next it is Emma. "I can't write 'bums' on my sign."

"Why not?"

"It seems insulting. I thought about 'alcoholics' and 'ex-mental patients' but they sound so mainstream. What should I do?" She is stricken with indecision.

"What about 'derelicts'? Or 'lay-abouts'—that has a nice nineteenth-century sound to it." Robin is feeling helpful again.

"I'll just avoid the whole thing. My favorite way out."

"You'll carry a blank sign?"

"I'll say 'Join Us.' That's positive. Or 'Keep the Rich Away.'"

"From what, the planet?"

"Exactly. 'Keep the Rich Away from the Planet!' Will anyone understand that?"

"You can explain it."

"As they panhandle me?" Emma is cheerful again.

Last is Maybellene. "There are cop cars everywhere," she whispers.

"Hello. Yes." Robin can hear heavy breathing from the phone. He is hoping it is a dirty phone call.

Maybellene's voice rises a hair. "Four cop cars are in front of the Men's Shelter. They are swarming, swarming, do you hear me," her voice rises several decibels, "everywhere."

"Maybe they saw our flyer. I knew we shouldn't have called ourselves 'The Gang to Keep the Rich out of the Neighborhood.' We should've been a committee. I told Barnaby that. Committees are much more respectable than gangs."

"There's a limousine pulling up in front. God, a fucking limousine."

"Oh, no. They're showing themselves in the daytime now."

"Some men are getting out."

"Probably real estate developers looking over the property."

"They are taking fucking pictures. Some man in a suit is smiling at a bum, smiling at him and getting his picture taken."

"Must be a politician."

"He's leaving."

Robin is overwrought. He grabs a joint and gets high. Maybellene is panting into the phone, forcing her eyes to scan the street for any sign of what it might mean.

"I'll go down to the street and snoop. I'll call you when I find out something. Call everyone."

"They're all calling me."

She leaves the building looking normal and composed. The first cop she meets, she bats her eyelashes ever so slightly at and asks sweetly, "What is going on here anyway, Officer?"

The man glances at her and growls, "What are you doing on this street?"

"I live right there," she says, batting her eyelashes a little harder. She points to a door which looks like no one would be safe living behind.

"Rough street. You ought to be careful."

'He's being protective,' she thinks. 'The old eyelash trick is working again.' "What happened?"

"Some gas lines broke or something in that rat hole last night and some guys died."

"From the gas?"

"Probably too drunk to smell it or to move. This City Hall guy's come down here to say they're gonna clean this joint up."

"That's terrible. It's frightening what goes on around here." She knows she has found just the blabbermouth she needs, and on the first try. 'What good luck.' She moves in for the kill. "So you'll be leaving here as soon as you clear everything up?"

"Oh, yeah. They took the bodies away already. We're just waiting for the word to leave."

"Oh, I forgot my money. How silly of me. Thank you, Officer." She turns and walks back to her apartment triumphantly. She calls Robin and tells him what she has learned.

"So we're going to demonstrate to keep a death trap open?"

"No action is perfect."

They are all expected at Maybellene's by four o'clock. Emma arrives first, dressed as her namesake, Red Emma, in steel-rimmed glasses, hair piled on top of her head, a long skirt, a wool jacket and sensible shoes. She hides her sign under clothes so no one will suspect.

"The streets are teeming with unfortunate men," she announces as she comes through the door. "I was panhandled four times, but nobody made a pass at me. That's encouraging, don't you think?"

"These are the only men I ever met who'd rather have a quarter than a fuck," Maybellene answers knowingly. She is in her bag lady outfit. Her eyes are black with kohl so she looks like she has just emerged from a bar brawl; her white hair stands up on end as if an electric shock has just passed through her body. She wears four skirts of various lengths and colors, two blouses and three sweaters that barely cover her because they are so full of holes. There are shopping bags filled with newspapers sitting around the room. While Emma is pulling her sign out from under her dress, Susan B. leaps into one of the bags and takes a shit.

"Stink, stink. Oh, no. Get out of there." Maybellene turns to Emma apologetically. "She's so political. She wants to be a part. I'll save this one to hurl at the cops if they show up."

They have settled down to a cup of coffee when Ruby waltzes in. He hasn't shaved in days, nor washed his hair nor bathed. He found his outfit in the garbage and decided not to wash it.

"You smell," Emma says.

"Since I stopped bathing I have been getting laid like crazy. The smell turns them on," he brags. "Oh, I hear you're ready for a little bounce around, make a baby or two."

"I changed my mind," Emma answers stuffily, trying to get a better whiff to see if she might get turned on.

Bruce arrives complaining of a sore ear from too much telephone.

"Be grateful so many think so much of you that they will put out the energy it takes to dial your number."

Rosa arrives at exactly four o'clock though he had been told three. He is wearing three pairs of long underwear covered by a ratty woman's fur coat. He immediately opens the coat to reveal that the underwear has been tie-dyed. It is a mass of purple and orange streaks so faded it looks dirty rather than colorful.

"Tie-dyed. Do you remember? Can you believe?" He swirls around. "Oh, my, the streets are teeming. You'd think people would stay home on such a chilly day."

"They are at home," Emma says icily.

"Where is Robin?"

"He's coming with Barnaby."

"Well, we might as well." Maybellene gathers up her bags and looks significantly at the others. Emma's stomach turns over as she hauls herself up.

"Let's go. Keep the signs hidden till we get down there," Rosa advises.

A bitter wind blows down East Third Street. Men huddle in every available doorway with bottles of cheap wine, trying to keep from freezing.

A small cluster of their friends from the bar wait in front of the Shelter looking like they are sure they have come to the wrong place. They all shriek at each other, delighted not to be alone. As they are forming a circle on the sidewalk, Robin and Barnaby appear carrying a video camera and a microphone. They are dressed as normally as possible—Barnaby in a leather jacket and dirty Levi's and Robin in dirty Levi's and a down jacket which makes him look like he has just gained thirty pounds, all of it above the waist.

"The press! The press!" they shout and immediately feel important. A chant starts.

"Bums, bums, we're all bums.
Keep the rich on the run."

The men on the street are incredulous. "Man, I have to give up drinking," one puffy, red-faced man says to another one who is so full of Thorazine that his eyelashes brush his shoes.

"What're they saying?" another slurs to a companion who is sprawled out on a mattress on the sidewalk. He raises his head for a look. "I think it's a fashion show," he says and drops back onto the mattress.

"Bums, bums, we're all bums.
Keep the rich on the run."

"Speak for yourself," a man yells at them. He pulls himself into a dignified position and mutters, "Who they calling bums .

anyway?"

Other men, less far along in their daily inebriation, spot the fun and stroll over. Robin falls into the line next to Rosa.

"It looks good. I really cased the place when I got my check today," Rosa whispers.

"Don't tell me a thing."

"But it's so exciting."

"If they torture me I won't be able to betray you."

He moves quickly next to Emma. "Where is Scarlet?"

"She was afraid she'd get kicked in the stomach."

"The people around here can barely stand up."

"She doesn't waste her energy marching for men."

"This is about the right to be poor and survive."

"There's no such right as that." Emma is getting peevish. Robin knows Scarlet's arguments have gotten to her. He also knows she hates demonstrations. She is here only out of loyalty to her friends and guilt about her relative privilege.

"Let me see your sign." She turns it towards him. It reads, "Make the Shelter Safe."

"Good choice."

Men pour out of the Shelter to watch the show. Soon they are surrounded by what looks like hundreds of shabby, down-and-out men. Three bag ladies lean against the wall of the Shelter making loud comments on the sad state of American manhood.

Someone starts "Save the Shelter, save the poor" and the crowd picks it up. The street is getting clogged. Cars move slowly and finally have to stop. Horns blare. One car moves slowly, trying to brazen its way through the crowd. The chant bounces off the buildings, filling the street with a fiery sound. "Save the Shelter, save the poor."

Suddenly a loud siren blows a demand to be allowed down the street. The chant subsides, the signs vanish and everyone walks as naturally as possible away from the sound of the sirens. By the time the cops manage to get down Third Street everything looks normal, with everyone pretending to be in a stupor, though, for most, only a minimum of pretense is necessary.

In twenty minutes they all regroup in the bar where Scarlet, dressed in pink polyester pants and a pink polyester maternity top, is beating a Puerto Rican teen-ager at a game of pool.

"Oh, wasn't that fun?" Rosa exudes all over the bar. "Some of those drunks are so cute. One was cruising me heavy. He kept rubbing his crotch and staring at me."

"He probably had fleas."

"Or couldn't believe what he was seeing."

After a couple of drinks and a joint, Maybellene strolls to the pool table to have a talk with Scarlet.

"You stood me up today for drinks, Scarlet. Why?"

"I'm sorry, I completely forgot."

"We must talk."

"I know you disapprove, but my mind is made up." Scarlet flashes a sweet, fake smile at Maybellene, who returns it with a fake jab at her stomach.

"Child molester."

"Breeder."

"Not you too?"

"How will you manage?"

"Like all single mothers."

"Badly."

"With help from my friends."

"I hate kids."

"You'll love her. Just wait. I intend to do this." Scarlet is being so strong that Maybellene realizes she is no match for her.

"I'll give you what I can," Maybellene says sincerely, even though she has no idea what that means.

"Can't ask for more." Scarlet is relieved, knowing there is now one less friend to give her attitude.

"Let's play some pool."

Charlie stumbles into the bar stoned on weariness from work. "I just finished at the office. I guess I missed it, huh?" Everyone looks at him. The mood has turned somber.

"It was a fucking joke anyway," Barnaby growls. "The video camera didn't even work."

"So we won't even be in the movies?" Rosa asks glumly.

Bruce, feeling that Barnaby's mood is somehow about him, moves to the pool table to watch the game. Charlie is intimidated by Barnaby and looks to Robin for comfort.

"It wasn't the storming of the Bastille. But it was something."

"At the first cop siren everyone ran away." Ruby is upset at the missed confrontation. "It's like nothing even happened. Unless you riot, they don't know you're pissed off. We might as well just sit in the bar and forget the rest of the world."

Charlie thinks that's a nice idea so he settles down to have a drink.

Joints move down the bar. By the time the fourth one passes him by, Barnaby thinks, 'I feel better. Dope does it every time. It's the only way I can get through it all.' His mind drifts. Words surround him—alienation, anomie, nausea, disjointed— all words of discord, unhappiness. 'But they are only words. Things do still work, sort of. We are still here, sort of. No one has been killed. But then, no one has asked to be killed yet. If you are ready to be killed it is probably easy. The papers are filled with death. And the military is arming the whole world. Every fascist in the world has enough lethal weapons to poison us all. It must be the end.' Barnaby begins to think that the death trip of those in power has become his trip. He leans slightly towards Robin and says, "They are preparing us for annihilation. They have everything at hand necessary to end us all. And I seem to be helping them."

"By being passive?"

"Yeah. I barely fight them at all. No one does. We all go about our lives like...I don't know, like it's all normal. Like atomic bombs and poisons spilling over the earth and torture and genocide are all normal. How can we go about our lives knowing what we know?"

"You can't know too much."

Barnaby knows that is wrong. "I know too much."

12

THE LIMITS OF COCKSUCKING

Robin feels sandpaper rubbing over his balls. He stirs, thinking he is dreaming. He feels it again. He reaches for his crotch and finds Auden sprawled out between his legs licking his balls.

"Auden. Get out of there." He begins to pull him up when a sharp claw catches in the flesh of his inner thigh.

"Yeahhh," he yells. Auden meows in protest and scampers away.

Charlie runs into the room. "Sweets. What happened?"

"Auden. He was after my balls again. He scratched me." Robin is pouting.

"Let me see." Charlie pulls the tangled covers off Robin and examines his inner thigh. He sits on the bed, leans over and licks the mark. Since his head is already there he puts Robin's cock in his mouth and begins to suck on it.

Robin's mind goes out of control. 'What is he doing? We haven't had sex in months. Why is he doing this? What does it mean? Do I need this? I'm not ready.' As his mind races along groves of doubt and mistrust, his body relaxes and suddenly he has an orgasm. Not a major orgasm, but still an orgasm. Charlie licks up all the juices, smacks his lips, kisses Robin on the cheek and says, "Thank you. That was yummy." He leaves the room to make breakfast.

Remembering he has to go to work, Robin groans his way out of bed, letting the walls hold him up all the way to the bathroom. He opens his eyes and looks directly at his rounded tummy, his slightly drooping pecs and the hint of bags under his eyes. He pats his stomach. "My little Buddha belly," he murmurs.

Charlie calls, "Breakfast." The toast is burnt and the eggs overcooked but Charlie is so effervescent that Robin has to laugh and relax.

"How did *Too Much Heat in the Amazon* go last night?" Robin inquires.

"Except for the fact that Jane Jordan, our leading drag queen, forgot half his lines again, a door fell off its hinges, half the plants died so it looked more like the Nevada atomic test site than the Amazon and a member of the audience fell asleep and snored loudly, it went O.K. When are you coming to see it?"

"Closing night. By then everyone should at least know their lines."

"Well, if people keep up what can only be called a highly organized boycott, that might be very soon."

"Keep me posted. Got to run. Nice breakfast. Soon."

The Staten Island Ferry is nearly empty. Robin finds a seat on the top deck and settles down with the *Times.* He reads through several pages of disasters, international conflicts and war preparations all presented in a style so bland and neutral that he thinks he is reading about county fairs and dog snatchings when he realizes that the seat of his pants is damp.

"Goddamn it," he mutters and jumps up. He has sat in a small puddle of cold hot chocolate. A large woman with bleached hair gives him a sympathetic look. 'I guess I can't turn my back to the class today,' he thinks, resolving to keep a change of clothes in his office.

He finds another seat, inspects it, and sits down to read about more pending catastrophes posing as minor irritations to the good life. They have suppressed a magazine article on how to make an H-bomb, even though all the information needed to make an H-bomb has already been published. 'I guess they don't like it all in one place,' he thinks. Leaks in the West Valley nuclear waste storage facility are reported. 600,000 gallons of radioactive liquid have eaten through the inner walls of their containers and are now working on the outer walls. Forty pounds of plutonium, enough to kill everyone on the planet, is missing from a Kerr-McGee plant in Oklahoma. 'How do you carry plutonium around?' he wonders. 'Surely not in a suitcase.'

He searches for some good news. Finding none, his eyes glaze over and his mind fogs up. Then he notices a story about how the TVA, for the last twenty years, has been making building blocks from radioactive sludge so that now thousands of homes in the South are permanently radioactive. He realizes how lucky he is to be living in an old slum building put up before a malevolent science split the atom.

Feeling almost smug about his good fortune, his eyes drift to an article detailing the sudden rise in membership of the Ku Klux Klan. 'It's the CIA. It fits perfectly.' He tries to reconstruct the CIA scenario he has recently discovered. He wants to tell his class about it. 'The population gets restive, riotous, rebellious and, finally, revolutionary. Or it gets lazy, laconic and liquor-laced. In either case the people don't work at top efficiency for low wages. Profits are not what they could be. The government, trying to be useful to the profit seekers, promotes any right-wing terrorist group it can find. They attack the people, the government calls them names and the people fight back. They have to. Otherwise they cannot live. The Klan is a natural for the CIA. Promote it and you promote civil war. As violence increases, the army is forced to step in to restore law and order. This is done by liquidating anyone who can be vaguely associated with the left. It can be a bloodbath, as in Indonesia, or forced migration, as in Uruguay, or mass arrest, killings and torture, as in Chile. Whatever the means, they end up with all the rebellious souls gone, the army in control, and the corporations in the money. The Klan's revival fits perfectly....'

His thoughts are interrupted when the boat slams into the dock, throwing one old man to the floor and signaling its arrival in Staten Island.

A cold wind comes in off the Bay, so he hurries to school. 'The air smells more rancid and the sky is darker than it was in Manhattan,' he thinks. 'But it always smells here in Cancer Alley,' he remembers to reassure himself.

113

As he walks into the building a guard yells at him. "What are you doing here?"

He reaches into his front pocket for his ID. It isn't there. He says, "I work here."

"School's closed today."

"Closed? What's the holiday?"

"Chemical dump blew up in 'Lizabeth, over in Jersey, last night. Everybody's been ordered to stay home."

"Oh, my nerves," Robin mutters. "What am I supposed to do?"

"The best thing would be to stop breathing." The guard chuckles at his little joke. "But since you can't do that, I'd cover my nose and mouth with something and go home fast."

Robin is afraid he is going to cry. He can't tell if it is because of the poisoned air or his overwhelming feeling of helplessness. He goes into a bathroom, takes off his jacket, flannel shirt and his Emma Goldman T-shirt, wraps Emma around his face, puts his shirt and jacket back on and runs to the ferry terminal building trying to breathe shallowly.

During the ride back on the nearly empty boat he sits on the lower deck, stares gloomily at the orange sky and thinks about the fire bombing of Dresden and the extermination of homosexuals in Nazi concentration camps.

At home he is restless. He feeds the cats and sweeps the bedroom. He walks aimlessly from one room to another. It is dark but still early. No one will appear at the bar for at least three hours. He suddenly hates all his records; he cannot bear to reread *Christopher Street* or *Mother Jones*; he can only find kiddy rock on the radio and there is no hot water. 'Maybe a cold shower would help.' The thought does not move him.

He lies on the sofa, stares up at the ceiling and counts the cracks in the plaster. Suddenly he lunges up from the sofa and dashes to the refrigerator. 'I'll eat.' A jar of mayonnaise, a dried pickle on a piece of waxed paper and a half empty bottle of beer stare back at him. 'O.K., relax. Read a good book. Go to bed. The day's over and it's been a bummer but no one got killed that you know of, so relax.' He makes three phone calls but no one is at home. 'It's freezing outside. Where can they be? Probably all together someplace having a good time.' He calls Scarlet to warn her about the Jersey poisons in the air. There is no answer.

'I'll devote myself to the cats. They need me.' He undresses, putting on a torn terrycloth bathrobe, and settles once more on the sofa. He invites Auden and Gloria to join him, which they do only after he gets up and gives them both some more food, which they eat ravenously.

As the cats settle down he stares at the wall trying to black out his mind, hoping time will pass. An old mantra enters his mind timidly. He tries to encourage it but pictures of chemical dumps exploding and dead birds keep intruding. 'Maybe Barnaby's right. We know too much. How can a person relax, let alone be happy, knowing so much?'

The phone rings. He is relieved. 'I don't care who it is,' he thinks. He disentangles himself from the cats and answers, "Hello."

"Oh, you sound so sexy," Barnaby says.

"Depressed would be closer."

"Cheer up. I have a new idea for you." He hesitates for effect. "I just figured out why I'm queer."

"Whatever brought that up?"

"Well, I was sitting in the men's room here at work, getting stoned, and I started thinking about how strange it is to be queer, this thing that nobody ever wanted you to be, that everyone wishes you weren't, and it came to me."

"Yeah?"

"It was God that did it."

"Barnaby." Robin is alarmed. "Maybe you should go home. You may be working too late today."

"No, no. It's simple. God, who is the main man after all, has this son who he allows to be tortured to death by other men. I never forgave God for letting that beautiful man be treated like that. I mean he is God, he could have stopped it. But no, he lets them do terrible things to his only son. It really turned me off. I

115

never wanted to have anything to do with men who acted like that."

Robin squeaks, his mind races. "Of course. It was my father who turned me queer. Turned me right around. Not just him though. All the men I knew as a kid. Men turned me queer. Maybe that's the same as God doing it. He is just like all the men, only more so, and all those men were so scary. My father and the other grown-up men were always away at work or on the golf course or in a bar. And everywhere I saw them they were always trying to do each other in. I would hear who came in first and who came in last after each golf game. The losers were always ready to blast or cream or obliterate or beat or stomp the winners the next time. It made me very nervous. No, more than that. I was afraid. I was afraid of these men. Why would they let me live, let me get to be a grown-up? I'd only be another person to beat."

Echoing Robin, Barnaby remembers. "I felt that same way about the other boys my age. They were always completely impossible. Arrogant, competitive, violent, rowdy, loud, full of practical jokes to humiliate me and punches and slaps and kicks. Whenever the adults weren't looking, of course. I wanted to love them to calm them down. I wanted to kiss them to take their minds off their hostility toward me."

"Oh, me too." Robin is excited. "I knew if men just sucked each other off, they would stop beating each other up. And I was right. I was this young kid, barely able to navigate a small town and a small family, yet I had this amazing knowledge. So I became a faggot. And for thirty years I have been going to bath houses and bars and bushes and beaches filled, often crammed, with men. And they are not violent with each other."

"Growing up I used to crave, I mean crave, straight men. That was all there were, after all. I can still feel it in whiffs walking down the street, seeing a straight man walking towards me. There's that desire to disarm him by going to bed with him, or not even that, a wink would do, a flirtatious smile, a quick move of the hand to his crotch, a wiggle of his ass, a sign that he liked me, that we needed each other in some way."

"Faggot sex might just lead to the elimination of war,"Robin says, amused by the notion.

"That's probably why the generals hate us so much. We could put armies out of business."

"I can see the headline now. 'Cocksucking Destroys the Pentagon.'"

"So we finally have a concrete suggestion for stopping nuclear war."

"Get all men sucking cock." They both squeal with delight.

"Barnaby, sometimes you are as good as a joint for my head."

"I love you too. Got to go. I must look busy. Kiss, kiss."

Robin bounces around the room, delighted by his new idea. He puts on a Holly Near record and sits down to explain to the cats, who slept through the conversation, why he is queer.

The phone rings. He picks it up and hears purring. He puts the receiver next to Auden's ear. Auden rolls over to get away from it.

"It doesn't even turn the cat on."

"Ah, baby," Ruby moans, "I'm out here in Queens in my father's house. You know how horny I always get when faced with my parents. Why don't you come out here and take care of your boy?"

"Honey, this beauty is off duty. Besides, I thought you'd be out robbing stores and bumping off the ruling class."

"Soon. When the time is right. It's all planned. No problems there. But I've got a problem here. Aw, come on. Listen to me. Nice blow job, pinch your tits hard, slap your ass. Doesn't that sound nice? Worth a subway, right, any day?" Ruby purrs again.

Robin is charmed by this offer. "How about a little foreplay? Just to get us hot."

"Like?"

"Like some kissing and licking and undressing. You do

know about foreplay, don't you?" They have not made love in several months. Talking dirty over the phone is as close as they get these days. Sex for them has always been a dramatic event. It usually occurs in several acts and has a theme. At first, ten years ago, it had been Ruby seducing Robin. It was fun. Robin was the most militant faggot in the community and Ruby was the wild, beautiful, straight, Italian street punk running amok. The incongruity of it delighted them both. After many months of this, it turned into Robin turning Ruby into a proper fag, a project that took several years of experimentation before it was abandoned as hopeless. Ruby did learn to suck a cock, Robin's, without throwing up or even gagging. He learned to get fucked without crying. And he even learned how to fuck without acting like a man. But he somehow never captured the feel of fag or at least never to Robin's satisfaction.

"So you're going to leave me here horny in Queens."

"I already got a blow job today."

"In some scuzzy toilet?"

"I do have a boyfriend, in case you've forgotten."

"Oh, the one you don't have sex with."

"Yeah, that one." Robin is slightly annoyed to have to think about Charlie's blow job and if it means anything or not. "School was closed today. A chemical dump in Jersey blew up and poisoned the air."

"I heard about that. I wondered if you would survive. How is school anyway?"

"It's a drain. I talk, but I'm not sure anyone listens. They do talk sometimes but they don't want to commit themselves. No one has stood up and declared themselves to be anything."

"No fags, huh?"

"Well, who knows? I suspect a couple. But no one has come out. In fact, no one has come out as a leftist or a feminist or even a right winger. I'll have to talk about abortion soon. That always makes people take a stand."

"Maybe they're comatose."

"I think they are intimidated by authority, even as

ludicrous an example of authority as me. Or maybe they are just tired from their lives—families, jobs and school. And poor. It's too much. Someone fell asleep in my class the other day and I was talking about pornography."

"Did you show any?"

"No."

"Well, no wonder. Who wants to hear you talk about it when the real thing is just around any corner? Or right here in my parents' living room."

"Where are they?"

"Out eating. My pants are down and my cock is beginning to move with the rhythm." Ruby's voice laughs over the wires.

"Masturbation is the best sex, I've heard." Robin would walk to the next room to see this hot picture but he would not take a subway to Queens.

"It takes two."

"Not if one of them has to schlep to a foreign country. So just breathe heavy and I'll be happy." Sarcasm about sex feels good to Robin. Make fun of it. Everyone, certainly him, takes it so seriously. Unless you are with a stranger, then it can be done as casually as eating supper or shopping for new shoes. But by the second date sex becomes fraught with meaning and importance. Since Ruby can't keep a hard-on very long, he has always treated sex more lightly than Robin. Robin appreciates this.

Ruby laughs and says, "It's going limp. Your rejection is not turning me on. Oh, no, maybe that means we're finished."

"We finished a long time ago. We are just mopping up now. You sleep good."

"I kiss the phone." Kiss, kiss can be heard.

The moment he hangs up Robin regrets his harsh rejection of Ruby's offer. He shivers. He gets up and walks to the radiator. It is cold. 'I ought to go to bed,' he thinks as he takes off his robe and dresses. 'A good night's sleep would be useful,' he thinks as he runs down the street to the Terminal Bar. He sees that the plywood window has become a graffiti battleground.

"Cocksucker" and "Motherfucker" predominate. In one corner he notices scrawled, "Faggots are nigger lovers." Gratefully, he sees someone has replied, "You bet we are."

It is nearly empty, but filled with so much smoke that his eyes water at once. Emma, dressed all in black, leans against the bar talking to Barnaby, dressed all in black. Robin notices Maybellene and Flow in a dark corner either making out or snorting coke. It is hard to tell which.

Barnaby reaches out for Robin, pulls him swiftly into his arms and gives him a lot of tongue. Robin surreptitiously glances around to see if Bruce is there, knowing Barnaby's passion is often calculated. He is not, so Robin returns the tongue. Robin and Barnaby are soon smacking their lips and wiping their chins.

"What are friends for if they can't give each other a little tongue now and then," Emma observes with only slightly suppressed jealousy. Robin goes for one of her ears and Barnaby for the other. They nibble her lobes and wet the inside. She laughs and pulls away. "Let's keep the heterosexuality to a minimum."

"If it's more than two people it's an orgy and orgies are correct," Barnaby announces.

"I came here only to get warm, but maybe I'll have a drink now that I'm here," Robin says, fooling no one.

"I came here to pick someone up," Barnaby says, leaning heavily onto the bar.

"This is not a cruise bar," Robin answers disdainfully. "If you want to do that sort of thing, go to the West Village."

"I would have, but I can't walk that far." He slouches onto a barstool.

Remembering the tongue kiss, Robin asks, "I thought you were off sex. You couldn't suck off the oppressor. Isn't that what you said last week?"

"I decided that phallic worship in the abstract is destructive, but phallic worship in the concrete is the best."

Robin laughs and kisses his cheek. "The men are definitely

out of control. You'd better get back out there on the street and try to calm them down. Did you hear that one of their chemical dumps in Jersey exploded today? School was closed. The air was so bad that I was told not to breathe it." Emma, engrossed in watching three other women in the bar, hears "chemical" and "explode."

"Scarlet is very upset," she says, remembering her long afternoon trying to soothe Scarlet.

"You saw her?"

"We went to see *China Syndrome* together, which may not have been such a good idea. That and the chemical drum got her pretty nervous."

"Was the movie scary?"

"Yeah, I guess. But it was a rather old, tired story. One good man, among all the bad men, comes forward to save us all from their fuck-ups."

"And Jane. Wasn't she doing anything?"

"Sure, helping the one good man."

"You don't think there are any good men left, do you?"

"Well, certainly not in any positions of power. They were all fired or quit or got killed a long time ago." Emma drains her scotch and water and orders another.

The piece of plywood that serves as a door flies open to reveal Rosa pulled up to full regal size. He stands for a moment and then announces, "I have just been mugged." Before they can go to him, he walks, as stately as possible, up to the bar. "A double scotch and a Quaalude," he orders. The bartender pours the scotch and Barnaby hands him a Quaalude. "It was unreal."

"What happened?"

"I'm in shock."

"Tell us."

"You'll never guess."

"Right you are, so..."

"I'm out walking, looking over my ex-employer's establishment..."

"You weren't."

"No. That comes later. I was just keeping my eyes open when this man asked me directions to the West Village. Innocent enough, right? So, since I was finished scouting I offered to walk him there. He was quite hunky and clearly in need of guidance."

"Always Lady Bountiful."

"While we were walking, he's telling me how horny he is, how he loves to get his cock sucked, though, he maintains emphatically, he's straight. Well, I've heard that one before so I suggest a small alley off West Street."

"An alley?" Emma is alarmed.

"It's dark and private there. Right off the street though. So he says 'Sure' and we go and I go down on him and he groans and moans and comes like crazy. And then, honey, he goes down on me, sucking like mine's the last dick in New York City. I came, exploded, I should say, and am thanking him and pulling up my pants when he pulls a knife on me." Robin's stomach sinks. Emma gasps. Barnaby closes his eyes, waiting for the gory part. "I was speechless. Money, he wants. So I give him my money, of course. He's not satisfied. He makes me empty my pockets. He takes my keys, my ID and my drugs. Everything I need to get by. I asked for my keys back. And, it was too much, he spits on me and calls me a slimy faggot. I almost laughed, it was so ludicrous. I wanted to point out a few recent events to him but figured this was not the time for a therapy session."

"And then he left?"

"Yeah. Backed out of the alley, leaving me with my pants down and dazed."

"Does he know where you live?"

"No. The ID had a San Francisco address on it."

"I have a set of your keys with me in fact." Emma feels very much to the rescue.

"He must have been from out of town," Barnaby grumbles.

"New Jersey, he said."

"Figures."

Rosa feels calm, almost cheerful. "Compared to that time in San Francisco when that maniac broke into my apartment, tied me up, forced me to eat all my drugs and then threatened to kill me, this seems mild."

"Just another chapter in the memories," Emma sighs, wondering who she can get to walk her home.

"I'm too freaked out to live," Robin explodes. "Give me a Quaalude quick." He clutches Barnaby's arm, pleading for a fast fix. He turns to Rosa, "My whole reason for being a faggot, which I just figured out today, in a profound talk with Barnaby, has just been blown to dog shit." He gulps his white wine and feels the pill hit his empty stomach. "I suck men off to disarm them. And now you're telling me it doesn't work."

"Just stay out of dark alleys and you'll do fine," Emma comforts.

He turns to Barnaby, needing love. "I suck cock to calm men down, so they won't be violent and hurt me. I thought universal cock sucking would bring universal peace."

Emma is incredulous. "You've been doing too many drugs."

"I can't live." Barnaby's arm encloses Robin. He feels safe. He hears, "Wait. The pill will revive you."

They spend the next two hours drinking as fast as they can, trying to calm down so they can figure out if Rosa should have known and how Rosa could have known that that man was trouble. A relaxed, playful, drunk feeling overtakes them. It is only then that they notice that Maybellene and Flow have snuck out.

"Where'd they go?"

"Who knows. To sleaze out someplace, no doubt."

Liquor and dope keep appearing. Robin walks to the bathroom and has trouble finding his way back. Emma trips over something invisible while she is standing still. She apologizes. Rosa forgets where his coat is and panics. It is in his hand. Barnaby tells the bartender, "I want a drink to go."

The bartender replies, "You'll be lucky to get *yourself* to go."

Rosa leaves, feeling like the robbery was a dream. Barnaby
and Robin walk Emma home so she can hold them up while
they protect her.

Without Emma, Barnaby and Robin cling to each other,
both lurching about on the sidewalk. When they reach their
parting point they lean against each other and kiss passionately.

"We shouldn't do this right on Second Avenue," Robin
cautions.

"If they can't take a joke, then fuck 'em," Barnaby answers
in the toughest tone he can manage.

13

THE CENTER DOES NOT HOLD

The heat is still off and the water is still cold. Robin goes to school unwashed, unshaven and in a rotten mood.

He called and heard that the place was open. 'I guess all the poison has blown to Long Island. But it can't be safe there yet. They are forcing me to breathe noxious fumes if I want my paycheck. Die to survive.' He thinks how workers in coal mines, textile factories and chemical plants are poisoned every day they work. 'I thought being a college teacher was going to be safe.' He laughs, even though he knows the joke isn't that funny.

On the ferry boat he makes a resolution. 'I will lay low for a couple of days. I'll lead my life like a normal person. I'll go to work, have cocktails, eat in restaurants, and watch TV. I won't talk about anything heavy with anyone and I'll unplug the phone. I'll just pretend that everything is going nicely and that it will all last forever.'

He braces himself before entering his first class. 'I won't keep them long,' he decides. When he walks in, with a sly apologetic smile on his face, the room is in an uproar. His mood lifts at once.

"Did you hear?"

"We had to stay in our houses for two whole days."

"They sent trucks around with loudspeakers blaring, 'Stay inside your homes. Do not breathe the air outside.' What about the air inside? That's what I want to know about."

"My daughter is throwing up now for two days. The doctor says it will pass when the air clears more. How the hell does he know?"

"My whole family is shut up in the house for two long, long days. My marriage nearly broke up."

"What prevented it?"

"My husband finally locked himself in the basement. I pretended he was at work."

"My kids said they saw something like it on TV, so they thought it was a rerun."

"I haven't smelled clean air in so long I couldn't tell the difference."

Robin thinks about Emma Goldman and how she would know the right things to say to start them all marching on Elizabeth, New Jersey. He manages to say, "Let's talk about greed and capitalism and the poisoning of the earth." He is dancing in front of the blackboard with excitement.

"But the rich have to breathe the air too, don't they?"

"They all live uptown."

"It's the same air."

"They have country places."

"Maybe they don't care as long as profits stay high," Robin suggests.

"Come on. They can't be that stupid. What about their kids?"

"They'll leave their kids enough money so that they can move someplace else."

"Where they going to move to?"

"Maybe they don't care," Robin says again, realizing that his students are such decent people that they are having trouble imagining the overwhelming seductiveness that greed has for the rich. He tells them what he knows about the rich: their indifference to everything but money; their contempt for the not-rich; their belief that they are so smart and powerful they can take care of all problems they create. "They'll leave us here to breathe the poison air and drink the poison water and move on with the money. They don't care." He thinks of the black limousines in his neighborhood.

Two black women sit, quiet and cool, in the front row with slight grins on their faces. Robin knows them to be veterans of the racial struggles and wonders when they will join in.

Finally, one turns her entire body around to face the class and asks with obvious sarcasm, "You just finding all this out? It's been going on a long time and they won't change voluntarily. We have to destroy this rotten system and build us a new one." She turns around to face the front.

Her friend turns around and continues, "They're not going to wake up one day and say, 'Oh, my, how awful of us. We're sorry. We'll mend our ways.' They will only stop when we make them stop."

Her friend turns around again, smiling. "We have to stop them. Continuous sabotage. Learn whatever you can and then fuck with the system. Sit-in at the welfare office, scramble the banks' computers, be a sniper and get a cop."

The class erupts.

"You'll only hurt yourself if you mess with banks' computers."

"How they gonna know how much I got in the bank?"

"How much you got in the bank?"

"Not much. But enough for a rainy day."

"You better get it out 'cause it's pouring outside."

"Money is power," Robin says, looking for a generalization.

"And that's it. Everything and everyone is up for sale. You got the money you can buy your way into any place."

"It's the one thing left we don't talk about. Money." Robin feels good. "You can ask people about their jobs, their families and even their sex lives. But you don't ask them how much money they make. The rich hide how much wealth they have. They know if word got around about how much loot they have managed to steal from us, class warfare would break out. When one percent of the population owns thirty-five percent of all the wealth, you know some of us are not getting very much."

"Money is power," one of the black women says loudly. "Redistribute money and you redistribute power. And those who have are not going to let go of it if they can help it."

Her friend continues. "Look at all of you. Worried about

your savings accounts if the computers get fucked up."

"But it's all we've got."

"And there is a sad tale. It's all you got 'cause it's all they let you get." 'People are finally coming out,' Robin thinks, 'and it looks good.'

"You've got so little 'cause they've got so much."

"I barely have enough energy to work and take care of my kids. Where am I going to find the time to fight the system? They make it nearly impossible to survive."

"They arrest black folks even when we don't do anything wrong. You know how they treat black folks when they catch them actually fucking things up."

"They shoot first and ask questions later."

"They've got it all set up in their favor—the police, the courts, the newspapers, the banks. How you gonna fight all of that?"

The conversation moves to the difficulties involved in resistance, the sacrifice demanded of people who struggle for social change, the odds against success. The mood becomes more somber. Robin's euphoria fades as he realizes that his students feel overwhelmed and weary. They feel barely able to keep their own lives going and impotent to change America.

He feels too exhausted to face another class. When the secretary tells him that at least twenty students have called in to say they won't be there because they are afraid to leave their homes, he calls the second class off.

Sitting on the ferry, Robin is stricken by sadness. He looks at the gray, bleak sky and tries to remember his last acid trip when he had cried because the world looked so beautiful. But he can't bring it back. His mind fills up with images of starving bloated children and napalmed peasants and festering, polluted industrial landscapes.

He remembers he has to meet Scarlet for drinks at Lady Astor's. 'Do pregnant women drink liquor?' he wonders as he enters the red-velveted, crystal-chandeliered restaurant. He sees her sitting at the bar.

"You look great," he lies, kissing her.

She groans. "I feel like yesterday's puke."

"You did something to your hair."

"It's turquoise."

"I can see that. Are you drinking?"

"No. I'm nauseous; I have pains; I'm dizzy and I stopped eating."

"You ought to be home in bed."

"I have been for two days. I need to get out. If I faint, put me in a cab."

"So this is what being pregnant is like?"

"I hope not. Nine months of this and I won't have the strength left to push her out."

"You heard about the chemical dump in Jersey?"

"Yeah. Did you see it happen?"

"No. I got to Staten Island after it happened."

"What was Staten Island like?"

"Smelly."

"Oh, before I forget, here's the dope." She slips a plastic bag out of her purse and slides it under the bar into Robin's hand. He puts it in his pocket and gives her some money.

Trying to be cheery, he says, "Dish. Give me some dish."

"I guess you haven't heard about Barnaby yet."

"Heard what?"

"He was beaten up. I hear he was nearly killed."

Robin grips the bar so tightly that pains shoot up his arms. He opens his mouth to speak, but it is so dry nothing comes out. Finally he sputters, "When? I just saw him last night."

"It happened last night, that's all I know." They both stare off into space, too weak to continue. Scarlet rouses herself. "Maybellene called me. She's at St. Vincent's, but they won't let her see him."

"That's it?"

"That's all I know."

They are both near hysteria.

"It makes me scared. I should leave New York to have this

kid. I brought my mace with me today. Everyone on the street looks like a killer."

Robin looks around at the white linen tablecloths and huge mirrors and smartly dressed waiters, the velvet drapes and the crystal and silver on the table. His grip on reality slips a notch. He feels safe here. It all seems ordered and solid like it could last forever.

"My energy's gone. I'm sick and wary and scared." Two tears silently fall down her face. Robin notices and takes hold of her hands. They sit silently at the bar for a while. "I can't live with all this violence anymore. It's always been like this. My earliest memories are stories of pogroms and concentration camps and Jews being taken away in the night. My mother always said, 'We're safe here in America,' but who knew? How could she know? Who knows now? Women and dykes and hippies and radicals and poor people and everything I end up being . . . all subjects of violence. I can be raped, robbed, beaten, arrested, interrogated or tortured anytime some man decides to do it. It wears me down. I want to make life, but, Robin, I don't know." Her eyes are filled with doubt. Her body shakes slightly. "I'm a survivor, I know that. I just have to pull myself together." She offers Robin a weak smile.

Two tears roll down his face. He gives her a weak smile back. "Do you want to stay at my place for a little?" It is the only comfort he can think to offer.

"No. Thanks, though. I want to go home. Put me in a cab, O.K.?"

"Sure."

Robin walks home quickly. He fears that if anyone speaks to him or touches him he will scream. He undresses and crawls under the covers. The cats scream for food but he ignores them. He tries to masturbate but his cock does not respond to his hand. He tries a few old sex fantasies but he loses interest in each quickly. He wants Charlie to be home, to be here in bed with him, touching him. He feels abandoned by Charlie. 'We must have a talk soon,' he thinks. He gets an old mantra started. He calms down a little. Then images of a bloodied Barnaby invade his mind. He concentrates on the mantra with all his mental power, but the mantra cannot push Barnaby out of his mind. He calls to Auden, hoping for distraction. Auden leaps onto the bed. Robin coaxes him under the covers where he snuggles up against his arm. But soon Auden seems to remember an important engagement and struggles out from under the covers and runs off. He reaches over and turns on the radio. Gloria Gaynor is singing "I Will Survive." 'Well, that's something.' His mantra begins to put him to sleep.

Suddenly, the bare bulb in the bedroom ceiling flashes on. Robin sits straight up in bed.

"Oh, hon. I'm sorry. I had no idea you were here," Charlie says sweetly, turning off the overhead light and turning on a lamp.

"What time is it?"

"One o'clock."

"Oh, I slept the whole evening away." He lies down, pulls the covers around him and turns onto his stomach. Gloria, sleeping on the end of the bed, is forced to stand up, turn around four times before he can lie back down.

"You must have been tired."

"Depressed."

"Oh, why?"

"Don't be so cheerful about it."

"I'm sorry. I just happen to be feeling good." He sits on the bed and lays his hand on Robin's ass. "What's the matter?"

"Barnaby's been hurt bad, Scarlet was near death when I saw her, my students are defeated before it's begun and I never see you."

Charlie is not ready for this conversation. 'Maybe we can skip over this lightly,' he thinks. "The play will be over soon. Then we can have dates again."

"I get confused." Robin is not ready for this conversation either. 'I won't get heavy,' he thinks. Then he hears himself saying, "We never make love. We never go anyplace together.

We barely see each other. So I don't know what to call us."

"Maybe roommates." Charlie shrugs and gets up.

"But I don't want a roommate."

"What do you want?" Charlie feels confident now.

"I want a boyfriend."

"Which means?"

"A little sex . . ."

"I gave you a blow job yesterday. That's a little sex."

"It certainly is." They aren't looking at each other but each knows the other is smiling.

"So what do you want?"

"I don't know. Something."

"Do you want me home every single night waiting for you to say something that will amuse me?"

"That doesn't sound like fun."

"Do you want me after you for sex all the time?"

"That's not necessary."

"Do you want me to demand that you stop going to the bar all the time so we can be together?"

"Good God, no."

"Well," Charlie thinks for a minute. "I do love you, for whatever that's worth."

Robin rolls over and smiles. "That's worth something."

"Besides, you have so many boyfriends already. I can't imagine why you need more."

"Not so many."

"Ruby and Barnaby to name two."

"They're part-time boyfriends."

"So am I. Now you've got three part-timers. How many can you handle?"

Knowing he has been outmaneuvered, Robin throws off the blankets covering up Gloria, who slides off the bed and runs away. He gets up and grabs a pousse print robe off a hook.

"What are you doing?" Charlie, naked, lies down and pulls the covers over himself.

"I'm going to read. I'm wide awake."

"What're you reading these days?"

"Doris Lessing."

"I thought you'd read all of her."

"I'm rereading The Four Gated City. It matches my mood."

"Ah, apocalypse now."

"Apocalypse soon."

"Give me a hug and a kiss. I did say I loved you. That's worth something." The kiss is long and gentle and sweet.

"I love you too," Robin says. "But I still think our relationship is fucked up."

"No as much as the rest of the world."

Robin has been completely had and he knows it. He laughs. "That's true. Sleep well." He turns the light out and heads for the lavender sofa to read about the destruction of the planet and the end of civilization.

14

TERMINAL PATIENTS GET ALL THE BEST DRUGS

Robin hears bells. He rolls over and reaches for Charlie. No one is there. Bells again. He sees it is two o'clock. "Oh, shit." He rolls out of bed, trips on a shoe and lurches toward the phone. A dial tone. The bell again. He lumbers down the long hall, presses the button releasing the outside door, opens the apartment door and rushes back to bed.

"Robin? Honey. It's Maybellene Donit. Where are you?"

Robin groans loud enough for all the neighbors to hear.

She stands at the foot of his bed, regal as a queen. "I have just the thing for you." She reaches into her oversized bag covered with seashells and pulls out a small vial and a tiny spoon. "Now sniff this and we'll be on our way."

Robin does as he is told. "More. I need more. You can't imagine how much I need more."

"We all need more, dear. Here," and she shoves another tiny spoon under his other nostril. An involuntary smile crosses his face. "Now that's better." She smiles with satisfaction as she snorts a couple of spoons herself.

"I want some. Who has it? How much..."

"Relax. I bought you a gram of your very own. I know what a drug fiend you are. Pay me a hundred any day you wake up before the banks close."

"It's my favorite."

"It's everyone's favorite. But to afford it you have to be, at least, upwardly mobile." She sprawls on the bed and kicks off her pink wedgies. "I guess you forgot our lunch date?"

"I guess I did. But now we don't have to eat. We can just lie here and grind our teeth together."

"I saw Barnaby." Robin feels himself close up. He does not

want to hear about it. He's angry with Barnaby. 'But what for? Why should I be angry at him?' This emotion shocks him so much he resolves to hide it as best he can. Maybellene doesn't notice. "He looks dreadful. His head looks like they took a baseball bat to it, which they probably did. They had to sew his ear back on. He gets dizzy the minute he stands up. His inner ear is fucked up. Can't walk a straight line."

"So that's hardly new." The bitterness in his voice nearly gives him away. To cover, he quickly asks, "What happened?"

"He doesn't remember a thing. He remembers leaving you and the next thing he knew he was in St. Vincent's. Scary, huh?"

"I'll call him."

"He is not taking calls or receiving visitors."

"Why?"

"He's too freaked out to talk and too vain to be seen this way. It's too depressing. It could happen to any of us."

"It probably will."

"I'd rather be picked up and tortured by the CIA than be clubbed to death on the street like a baby seal. At least with the CIA you'd feel like you must have done something to deserve it."

"Don't talk that way. I'm superstitious." Robin leaps out of bed, full of energy. "Let's have some tea and apple juice in the living room."

Maybellene puts on an old Peggy Lee record and settles on the lavender sofa. Robin puts on the kettle. He finds two dirty cups in the sink. He turns on the hot water. Nothing comes out. He turns on the cold water. A dark brown liquid trickles out. "Ugh!" he yells.

"What?" Maybellene asks, coming into the kitchen.

"Look at that water."

"Mine was like that too this morning. Does yours smell?" He puts some in the dirty cup and smells. "Ugh!"

Maybellene smells. "Sewage. Just like mine. They probably ran out of water so they figured they'd give us sewage instead."

"Let's do something."

"Why don't you call up the mayor and complain to him."

"I'll call the health department." Five departments and seven phone calls later, Robin, nearing nervous collapse, hears a tired but polite voice say, "Sewage? Yes, we have been getting a lot of complaints. We're looking into it."

"What am I supposed to do?"

"I wouldn't drink it if I were you."

"I . . ." But no words come. He hangs up and falls deep into the sofa.

"Here, drink some apple juice and have another snort."

"We might as well be living in Cairo. Here we are in the center of the empire and nothing works."

"I hear they are moving the center of the empire to Houston."

"They wouldn't dare do that to me. Well, I won't go. I was not brought up to live on a swamp." Robin is recovering from his bout with the bureaucrats. Auden walks daintily on the back of the sofa, steps on Maybellene's shoulder and slips down her chest into her lap, purring. Gloria sniffs Maybellene's shoes. They are feeling cozy. "So what's new by you? How's your romance coming? You two snuck out of the bar the other night I noticed."

"And what a night we had. We went to Pete's. Or have you heard already?"

"No. Heard what?" He wonders, with an edge of paranoia, why he has not been informed.

Maybellene squeals with delight. "Hot shit, I get to tell it again. Well, you know Pete's Pleasure Palace."

"That dump on Third Street and Avenue A?"

"The one."

"I've heard of it. I've never been there myself."

"We went there. They have this little platform and the girls stand on it and strip and wave their cunts in the men's faces."

"Where are the men?"

"They sit on folding chairs right in front of the platform."

"Sounds charming," he says, trying for a tone of sophisticated decadence.

"It was quiet when we got there, still quite early. There were these two empty chairs right in front of the platform, so Flow and I sat down. And before I knew what was what, this lovely lady puts her snatch right in my face. I couldn't be rude." Robin has to agree. "Then another one goes for Flow and bang, before I could even order a drink, there we were, naked on the stage making it with these two women. Ah. We had a time for ourselves. They turned the music way up and we were rocking and rolling. Then a bunch of fags from the bar popped in and they couldn't believe it. They were screaming and carrying on. We had a ball."

"It was the art piece of your dreams."

"Precisely. And, oh, honey, those women were hot. All-night Sallys. They didn't stop."

"What did all the het men do?"

"I didn't even notice. I was flying. I felt as free as a man."

"And this was good for your romance?"

"It was the cement on the cake."

"You mean the frosting on the foundation."

"Precisely, the pearl in the chocolate mouse. Though she is a little intense for me."

"Too intense for you?" Robin tried to imagine what that could mean.

"She doesn't sleep much. She spent a lot of time living on the streets where you can't sleep if you want to survive. So even when she's asleep she is half awake watching for an attack. Speaking of an attack..." She leaps up and runs for the bathroom.

Robin is alarmed. "Are you O.K.?"

"Just a stomach virus or something. Those germs never let up," she yells from the bathroom.

"How is she intense?" Robin pursues the matter walking towards the bathroom.

"She calls me up in the middle of the night to tell me her plans for castrating rapists or blowing up J. P. Stevens."

"I thought J. P. Stevens was in the South."

"She found this address in the New York phone book."

"Makes sense."

"Or smuggling arms to Iranian women or shooting up porno stores or kidnapping Henry Kissinger."

"She and I should meet. I have a few ideas about Kissinger myself."

"These are all great ideas, obviously, but I keep telling her she can't do them by herself, she'll get caught and please save her plotting for the daytime when it is more likely that I will be able to cope. She just doesn't sleep enough. It gets her crazy."

She emerges with bright orange on her lips and kohl hanging from her eyelashes. "I must run. I have to go uptown."

"Whatever for?" To Robin, uptown, which is anything above Fourteenth Street, is another country. It is where some of those people who run the empire work and it always makes him paranoid to be there. He assumes uptown is crawling with thieves since that's where the money is and good thieves always go where the money is, at least that's what Willie Sutton used to say.

"I'm only going to Eighteenth Street. I have to see a woman about a rock 'n' roll band."

"Are you buying one or selling one?"

"Hopefully joining one. How's Maybellene and the Mother Lovers?"

"Already lead singer. You work fast."

"I have only one life to live; let me live it as a star."

"You are a star," he laughs.

"Oh, no kisses. All these nasty germs." She flies out.

The apartment is suddenly quiet. Determined to keep it that way, Robin unplugs the phone. He is suddenly paranoid. 'What if someone needs me? What if we have to leave the country suddenly.' He plugs the phone back in. 'What if we have to flee, indeed. Where exactly would we go?' He remembers reading recently that one fifth of the people of Uruguay fled from the terror of the generals after their coup. 'But where could they have fled to?' he wonders. 'Uruguay is surrounded by countries infected with the same terror, Brazil, Paraguay, Chile, Argentina, Bolivia. Maybe they went to Mexico. We could escape to Mexico. Sure. A bunch of drugged-out, left-wing, queer gringos. I'm sure Mexico can hardly wait.'

He walks to the kitchen and checks the water. Sewage. 'I better leave a note for Charlie,' he thinks, sitting down on the sofa. He feels good, in spite of all the bad news. He does two more lines of coke and begins to clean up the apartment. Flying from room to room, he throws out old papers, empties the wastebaskets and sweeps up old kitty litter. The water in the bathroom appears clean so he carries all the dirty dishes in and washes them hunched over the bathtub. 'This is the pits,' he thinks, finishing. To collect himself, he does two more lines. 'I won't be selfish. This mood is too good to waste on me alone. I must spread myself around among my friends.' He dresses, remembers to write the note to Charlie and leaves the apartment.

It is balmy outside. The bank thermometer says minus two. 'That thermometer never works. You'd think the bank could afford to get it fixed.' Swirls of wind dance the garbage around his feet. The street is jumping, winos panhandling, punks giving attitude and fags cruising each other. He stops to buy cigarettes at the bodega and everyone is smiling. 'It's either the drug or the weather doing this.' The Spanish man behind the counter wishes him a good evening. He thanks him, too effusively he thinks, and leaves.

The Terminal Bar is mobbed. He is alarmed. 'What does this mean? It has been discovered. Oh, hopefully not by the *Village Voice*.' He squeezes in, finds a hook for his coat and worms his way to the bar.

He looks around and realizes everyone he knows is there, except Barnaby. 'We could have hidden in the corner together.' He clutches his drink, trying to look at home. Anger at Barnaby

140

wells up in him again. Pushing it aside, he pushes through the crowd until he falls against Rosa, who is inhaling deeply from a hash pipe.

"I needed that. I have to calm down," Rosa says.

"Getting all excited again?"

"I promised myself I would not get too excited until at least one thirty."

"Can you hold out that long?"

"Not packed in here with all these sizzling men."

"Go over there and hang out with the dykes," Robin suggests, pointing to the pool table.

"Where do you think I got this hash? Oh, it's so great to have dykes and faggots in the same bar. Where else in New York City in 1979 does this happen?" Rosa is euphoric. "We can see right here in this sleaze pit evidence of an evolutionary leap forward. A new world is emerging before our eyes that will put the brakes on brutality, pull a veil over violence, stamp a clamp on competition, and foster friendships, honesty, and love. Hold my hand and we'll leap together." Robin, slightly embarrassed by Rosa's effusions, tries to grab his hand but is moved on by the crowd. He floats freely until he flaps against the bar.

Maybellene is saying, "I tell you it's too bizarre. Americans were happy, more than that, thrilled, when their kids stopped smoking pot and got into alcohol. It made them feel secure. Like the kids had come home. They'll be just like us now."

"Drunks."

"It's always gratifying when your kids see the virtue of your ways."

"What you brought me was great," Robin whispers.

"Tell me about it," Maybellene shouts back.

"Get a load of Jake at the end of the bar." Bruce nudges Robin and points. "He is chatting and waving his arms just like he would do if there were someone actually listening to him."

"The show must go on."

"Quick, hide me." Ruby falls in between Bruce and Robin and bends low.

"From who?"

"That one."

"What's his story?"

"He chews on cigarette butts. The other night I saw him dunk one in his wine glass and then eat it. I nearly threw up."

"You do have to work with what you've got."

"Oh, there's one I have my eye on." Ruby wiggles and puts on a smile.

"Which one?"

"With the overalls."

"Very country."

"Authentic. I've met him a few times. He and his boyfriend live out in the woods together, they have for years."

"Charming?"

"But it gets them crazy sometimes. So they hot-foot it to the big city. He does sex and his boyfriend does junk."

"And sex too?"

"Did you ever have a junkie come on to you? Junk and sex don't mix."

"In that case, I'm surprised the Christians aren't in favor of junk."

"It makes you feel too good for Christians to approve of it."

"Maybe we should all become junkies next, just for a change." Ruby thinks he has an idea.

"It's been done to death."

"It's too fifties for me."

"Have you seen Barnaby?" Robin asks so softly he hopes Bruce won't hear.

"I hear he is a little better," Bruce answers icily.

Scarlet appears with a joint. "I am not having my baby in the hospital," she announces. "I intend to deliver her at home with the help of a midwife. I will not go to the hospital unless I'm terminal."

"Why bother then?"

"Because terminal patients get all the best drugs. And I mean the best."

They laugh merrily. 'Was that funny?' Robin wonders, inhaling another joint.

"You feeling better?" he inquires of Scarlet.

"A little, but mainly I'm just pretending. I figured if I continued with that down head, I'd turn the kid into a depressive. So I'm trying to elevate my mood. Going up." She puffs on a hash pipe and hands it to Emma.

"Oh, why can't it be like it used to be?" Emma exclaims, rubbing her body from her crotch to her neck with one hand and holding the hash pipe with her other hand.

"Used to? When?"

"When we were all free and radical and together and one. When we knew what it all meant."

"I must have missed something."

"When was that?"

"In the sixties."

"In the sixties I was in graduate school trying to become a good professional."

"I was a Catholic and a Republican."

"I was in junior high school."

"Maybe it was the seventies," Emma persists.

"This is the seventies."

"Emma, maybe it never really happened."

"What difference does that make?"

"You can't be nostalgic for something that never happened," Ruby insists.

"I will have it yet," she says, using both hands to rub her body from her crotch to her neck.

"If I see it coming I'll let you know."

15

THE JOY OF STEALING

"I've got some bad news for you." Robin hopes he is dreaming. "Robin, wake up, honey. We've been robbed."

"Was anybody killed?"

Charlie laughs, "Of course not. We've just been robbed, that's all."

"We've been robbed?" Robin is beginning to understand.

"Yeah. Your typewriter is gone. I don't know what else. Did you have dope here?"

Robin tries to be awake and think but he feels so vulnerable that his body folds up as he pulls the covers over his head. He lies in a tight ball in the darkness. "There should be a couple of ounces of pot in the fridge," comes his muffled reply. He sneaks his hand out of the covers over the side of the bed, feeling, until he finds his vial of coke on the floor. 'That's safe.'

"They're not here now."

"Check the money in the top desk drawer."

"Gone." Charlie has a lilt in his voice.

"Are the cats O.K.?"

"They're sitting right here waiting for you to show your lovely body." Robin is not tempted.

"Is anything of yours gone?"

"No. They only took your stuff." Robin can hear satisfaction, maybe even glee, coming from Charlie. He throws off the covers and sits straight up to confront him.

"That's the pits. You're happy about my misfortune."

"I am not," Charlie protests, "I'm happy about my good luck."

"How'd they get in?" Robin climbs out of bed and grabs a robe.

"Through the kitchen window."

"That's impossible. They'd have to leap from the fire escape and then balance on a tiny ledge while forcing the window open."

"I guess that's what they did. I'll nail the window shut."

In the kitchen the window is open. A fern and a geranium lie on the floor in a pile of dirt and broken clay.

"They're plant killers too. Thieving plant killers. Don't they know every plant they kill reduces the oxygen supply? What are they going to breathe?"

"And then they just walked out the front door," Charlie points out, ignoring Robin's outburst.

Robin walks to the sink and turns the water on. It is the usual light brown. He smells it. "The sewage is gone. Did you know we had sewage in the sink yesterday?"

"I saw your note and wondered."

"And now this. Did you hear anything?"

"Nothing."

"Thank the goddess we didn't wake up. What would we have done?"

"Nothing, I hope."

"Lie there quietly and be terrified. So that's something. At least we didn't know it was happening."

"Ignorance is bliss."

"Ignorance is sanity. Oh, but how could they take the only three things I need to function—money, dope and my type-writer?"

"I never see you use your typewriter."

"It doesn't matter if I use it or not. It matters that it's there in case I want to use it," Robin moans as he cleans up the geranium and the fern, throwing everything into the garbage.

"The plants will live."

"I can't bear to have them around. They'd only remind me of my loss." Drama has replaced real life. Robin feels better. "Violated in my own apartment."

"It was probably your skeevy friends practicing for their

146

big heist. Have they done that yet?"

"Oh, please, who knows. And don't insult my friends. They're the only friends I've got." Robin decides to cheer himself up. "I am going to will myself to think only pleasant thoughts today. I will concentrate on how lucky you have been to be spared and how wonderful it must feel to be so protected by the great spirit."

Charlie laughs and leaves the room, saying over his shoulder, "I've got to get ready."

"For what?" Robin is following him down the long hall.

"Some of us work, you know. Mr. Monster expects me there this afternoon. Some kind of staff meeting or something."

"I will concentrate on the revolution now going on in Nicaragua to get me started in the right direction. Then I will meditate on drag queens fighting the police for three nights on the streets of Greenwich Village. And, to top it off, I will fantasize a general strike in America."

"You have a busy afternoon ahead of you. Got to go. Bye, love." A quick peck on Robin's cheek and he is gone. With his audience off to work, Robin is forced off the stage and back into the bed where he hides for several hours, only sticking his nose out occasionally to snort some coke. When the phone rings for the ninth time he gets out of bed, notices how stoned he is and answers it.

"It's Emma. How are you?"

"Aside from the fact that I was robbed last night of all my possessions, I'm fine."

"What do you have that anyone would want to steal?" Her mind quickly moves through Robin's apartment, checking.

"Only a few small precious mementoes."

"Were you home?"

"In bed. Asleep. We heard nothing."

"Oh, lucky you." Emma realizes she has given no sympathy yet so she gushes for a few seconds to make up for her bad manners. "I'm off to the bar to play some pool. Do you want to come along?"

Stalling for time, hoping to get himself oriented in time, Robin unthinkingly asks, "Did you hear about Maybellene's sex show?"

He hears Emma take a deep breath and then announce grandly, "I do not want to speak about it." She then continues, "I told her that I did not care what she did, or even with whom she did it, in the privacy of her own bedroom, but I thought it was reactionary and in extremely poor taste to let hets have a peek at what dykes do."

"I thought public sex was always liberating."

"The only positive thing about it all is that at least some people got laid this week."

"And you weren't one of those people."

"Not that I've noticed."

"And you are a wee bit jealous."

"I am not jealous. Well, you know how I hate to miss things. Not that I would have done anything like that."

"You're upset 'cause you weren't at least invited."

"Sort of. But I'm also upset that it happened. And, of course, I'm upset that you were robbed. But you know"—she becomes pensive—"everyone is getting poorer. And a lot of people were poor to begin with. Stealing is a way to share the wealth." Anticipating Robin's thoughts, she pushes on, "I know you are not rich and certainly not the enemy, but you must admit that..."

"Oh, I know. They can have it. It's only stuff and I have more of it than most people. And no one was hurt. Bad times these are."

"They won't get better either. Getting better is over." They both fall silent. Eagerly they end the conversation.

Robin is so rattled from the coke and the conversation that he goes to roll a joint to calm down. He remembers the robbery. There is no dope. He stares glumly into the garbage at the two mutilated plants and thinks about the destruction of the Amazon rain forest and the depletion of the earth's oxygen supply. He waters the other plants, apologizing to them for his

148

unnecessary discarding of two of their kind. Believing he has redeemed himself with the plants, he dresses for the bar. He remembers to think about the revolution in Nicaragua and perks right up.

Strolling down Second Avenue with an early warm breeze blowing soot into his smile, he notices a headline announcing a nuclear accident at some power plant. Walking on, he muses, 'I'm sure I'll find out about the end of the world from the *Daily News*.'

He enters the bar ready for something. It is nearly empty. Two local lushes lean against the wall. A dyke sits alone, looking sad. Two men with short hair, mustaches, plaid shirts, Levi's and work boots lean against the bar talking to the bartender. Various lowlife lurk in the shadows. Emma and Scarlet are laughing over the pool table.

"These holes are too small for those big balls," Emma shouts over Aretha screaming "I can't get no satisfaction."

Robin settles in at the bar and orders a white wine. The pay telephone rings. 'Strange. I didn't know the phone worked.' Scarlet beats the bartender to it by a split second.

"This is Maybellene Donit."

"Fancy that. This is Scarlet La Rue. How are you?"

"Have you heard there's . . ."

"What?"

"There's been an accident at a nuclear power plant in Pennsylvania. It might blow up at any minute. If the winds change we'll all be radioactive." Maybellene is shouting. Scarlet can barely hear her over the jukebox.

"What is it?" the bartender asks impatiently.

"It's Maybellene. Something about an accident and radioactivity."

"Oh, that." He is relieved. "It's in all the papers." He walks back behind the bar.

"Maybellene, come over here. I can't hear you." The phone goes dead. "Does anyone have a paper?" Scarlet yells at the nearly empty bar.

"Yeah. Here," one of the look-alikes at the bar hands her a copy of the *Daily News*. Robin and Emma begin to read over Scarlet's shoulder.

"I never heard of Three Mile Island."

"Me neither."

"I've got to get out of here." Scarlet shoves the paper at Emma and goes for her coat.

"Scarlet, relax, wait, what's wrong?"

"I am pregnant, in case you've forgotten, and if I'm radiated my daughter could have two heads." She is very frightened.

"But look here. The paper says the government says there is no danger."

"When was the last time you believed what the government said?" Scarlet snaps.

"1962, maybe," Emma admits sheepishly. "Come to my place. I have thick walls. We'll listen to the radio." Emma puts her arm around Scarlet and guides her out of the bar, handing Robin the newspaper and whispering, "Keep in touch."

Robin settles back at the bar and reads, "No health hazard...Worst accident yet...released radiation into the atmosphere...radioactive iodine will be in milk soon..." He hands the paper back to the men, realizing that they are clones, that's why they look alike. He stares into his white wine.

"Pretty grim, huh?" one of the clones says to him.

"Just another day in the decline and fall of the world."

"Yeah," he chuckles. "I'm Jeff. This is my friend Jim."

"Hi. I'm Robin."

"Quiet night here. Is it always like this?"

"No. Guess everyone is home in their fallout shelters eating dried pineapples."

Maybellene bursts through the door yelling, "Where is Scarlet?" She spots Robin and dashes to him. "She's got to know about this. She's got to hide her stomach."

"She knows. She went to Emma's where the walls are thick."

"I'll go there. Keep in touch." 'That phrase again. Maybe something important is happening,' he thinks. There are so many disasters, catastrophes, bombings, killings, slow leaks, explosions and accidents that it is impossible for Robin to focus for very long on any one of them. They race through his life, one hardly begins before another one starts. Each one leaves the same small message in his brain—you are one step closer to the end. He considers going home. 'If I'm going to be depressed, I might as well do it here,' he decides and orders another white wine.

As the night moves on, the bar fills up somewhat. Robin can hear snippets of conversation about "the accident," as everyone seems to be calling it, but he tries to close his ears to the world around him and focus on his kidnapping Henry Kissinger fantasy. He is happily going over the scene where Kissinger gives him the exact scenario of the overthrowing of Allende, naming names from the CIA, the State Department, the Pentagon, and bragging about how he orchestrated it all, when his earlobe is bitten. He swings around on his barstool to face three pathetic imitations of Mafia hit men.

Rosa pulls off his dark glasses and whispers lasciviously, "I love being a thief."

"You didn't."

"Of course we did. Nothing to it."

"How much?"

"Six thou."

"Where is it?"

"Hidden."

"Well, tell me what happened." Robin is so relieved that they are here and safe and so excited at the thought of someone else being robbed that he forgets where he is.

"In private, my dear," Rosa cautions, "I will reveal all of our exploits. The careful surveillance, the expert lookout by Bruce"—Bruce bows—"the slick entry by myself and Ruby"—Ruby kisses Robin's cheek—"our top secret method for getting into the safe and the fastest getaway on record." He leans towards Robin. "Revenge on those who would dare to exploit Rosa Rugosa. Oh, it's so sweet. Drinks are on me."

Ruby cozies up to Robin, rubbing his crotch against Robin's leg.

"Crime makes you horny, huh?"

"You gonna love your daddy now that he's rich?" Ruby purrs as he mounts Robin's leg and begins to move back and forth. Ruby pulls Robin off his stool into his arms and sticks his tongue deep into Robin's mouth. They both moan. Robin gets a hard-on. Ruby reaches down and pulls on it a couple of times. "Is this for me?"

"If you think you can handle it."

"Try me."

"Drinks all around. Let's toast." Bruce puts a drink into Ruby's free hand and then gives one to Robin. Ruby holds on to Robin's hard cock.

"To sharing the wealth." They all drink.

"Ah, speaking of which, gentlemen"—Robin looks at them all very seriously—"my apartment was robbed last night. No one here was practicing, were they?" Ruby's grip tightens on Robin's cock.

"What could anyone possibly find to take there?" Rosa says imperiously.

"Dope."

"You weren't paid up. I warned ya." Bruce speaks in a heavy Italian accent.

"If I catch any of you typing..."

"Your typewriter? We gave that to Maybellene so she can write her memoirs," Bruce says, continuing the accent.

"What is this accent?"

"Part of my disguise. Does it sound crooked?"

"Kinky is closer," Rosa answers. "Where is Maybellene anyway?"

"She's at Emma's protecting Scarlet's stomach from radiation," Robin replies.

"Oh, that awful accident. They're doing it just to bring us

down on this night of our triumph over the bosses."

"Rosa, keep your voice down or I'll lower your lip to your shoes." The accent is almost convincing.

"Were you scared?"

"Oh, puff. What is fear where principles are concerned? So who is here tonight to play with?" Rosa swings around eyeing everyone conspicuously. He spots the two clones and gayly yells, "Are you two lost?"

They look at each other and answer in unison, "No."

"Well, if you want a tour of the sordid Lower East Side, I'll gladly show you the sights, such as they are."

"Rosa, don't tell anyone what happened. Remember our oath of silence," Bruce hisses into Rosa's ear.

"Dear, they're just two lonely clones, innocent wayfarers from Greenwich Village. They may never have seen a real queen before. I am just going to allow them to entertain me."

"Close your mouth or I'll tie your tongue up." Bruce pulls the collar of his black raincoat up over his ears.

"Oral bondage. Only you Mafia types would think of such a thing," he squeals as he moves towards the clones.

"Stupid cunt."

"Bruce!" Robin yells, offended. "You can be tough without being sexist."

"You can? How'd you do that?"

"Dykes do it all the time. Copy them."

"He wasn't being tough. He was being stupid like in 'too many knocks on the head' stupid," Ruby explains in defense of Bruce, who is looking penitent. "And it's impossible to be stupid and not be sexist."

Bruce takes off his dark glasses, slips out of his black raincoat and unbuttons his shirt down to his navel. "Now I'm a fag again." The accent is gone. "Oh, I hope Rosa keeps his mouth shut. Those guys could be FBI agents."

"Stop already. FBI agents never look that sexy," Robin says reassuringly.

"I have a nervous stomach." Bruce looks quickly around

the bar. "Has Barnaby been here?"

"No. I hear he's still in seclusion. Have you spoken to him?"

"No." Bruce looks dejected. He misses Barnaby and loathes him for being so cold lately. Only rejection ever breaks through his cynicism. When his lovers leave him, he sulks and pouts and curses and cries. It is only then that his friends know how much he feels. "I'm going home and feel sorry for myself," he announces, putting his black raincoat back on. He kisses Robin and Ruby good-bye and leaves the bar.

Ruby starts pulling on Robin's hard cock again. Robin pulls the front of Ruby's shirt out of his pants and runs his hands over Ruby's hard stomach and round pecs. "Let's go roll around naked on ten-dollar bills."

"The money's at your place?"

"Under the mattress. I'll shower you with it while I suck your cock." Robin figures that if he doesn't stop Ruby soon he will have an orgasm in his pants, so he agrees.

A cab is easy to find. They climb in the back and give the address to the driver. Ruby immediately grabs Robin into his arms and begins to kiss his neck and rub his cock. Robin tries to see if the cab driver is a fag killer but can see nothing through the bulletproof shield separating the front seat from the back. Robin pushes Ruby into the corner of the back seat. Ruby lies back, licks his lips several times and unzips his pants.

"If you take your thing out here, I'll bite it off," Robin warns.

Ruby laughs and sits up straight. "Next time I want you with me when I pull a job. We can fuck in front of the open safe."

"Anything for a little danger?"

When the cab arrives, the driver pretends that he does not speak English and refuses to look at them. Robin runs up the apartment stairs ahead of Ruby. He knows otherwise they'll be having sex in the hallway.

Ruby has a small three-room apartment. Clothes have

been thrown everywhere, dirty dishes lie in the sink, and records and books in piles. Ruby immediately sits at the table in the kitchen and rolls a joint.

"Smoke this."

"Do you have any to sell? I now have none."

"If you're good tonight I might just give you some."

Ruby leafs through a pile of records until he finds an old John Coltrane and puts it on. Robin slouches on a metal folding chair. Ruby walks up to him, kneels at his feet and takes off his shoes and socks. He lifts Robin out of his chair and takes off his shirt and T-shirt and sucks on his nipples. Robin pulls Ruby's shirt up until it is around his neck. He rubs his bare back, kneading his spine. Ruby raises up and they kiss and lick each other's necks.

"I bet money turns you on, doesn't it, baby?"

"Let me see how much and then I'll let you know."

Ruby shoves Robin back onto the metal folding chair, growling, "You men are all alike. You can't love a boy for his body. No, you want his money too." He leaps to the bed in the next room, rips off the mattress, scoops up handfuls of cash, dashes into the kitchen, springs up onto the table and throws the money into the air. "Get down and grovel for the dough."

Robin, realizing at last what the game is tonight, hits the floor and begins grabbing tens and twenties. Ruby jumps off the table and onto Robin. They roll around in the money until Ruby gets a hold on Robin's arm. He forces it up Robin's back until Robin goes limp. Then he reaches down and scoops up a handful of bills and stuffs the money down Robin's pants and then into Robin's half-opened mouth.

Robin spits them out. "They have germs."

"What do you care! It's real money." He spins Robin around, forces both of his hands into Robin's pants and begins rubbing money over Robin's cock. He pulls one hand out, undoes Robin's pants, which fall to the floor. He falls on his knees and carefully wraps Robin's cock in twenties and begins to suck on the tip while he jerks him off. Soon Robin comes in huge spurts. Ruby moves back and lets the cum fly out onto the money on the floor.

"You gonna lick that up?" Robin asks in a deep voice.

"Yes, yes," and he does, licking each bill clean of cum.

Robin stretches out on the money-covered floor. He grabs bills and puts them over his body. He sees a fifty. He holds it out to Ruby. "Take your clothes off and sit on my face." Ruby takes the fifty and holds it between his teeth. He stands up and undresses, slowly, moving his hips to the music. Naked, olive-skinned with light hair on his chest and a hard cock, he stands over Robin. He takes the fifty out of his mouth, rolls it up, licks it, and sticks it into his asshole. Slowly, still in rhythm, he lowers his cock, balls, and ass onto Robin's face. Robin reaches for the fifty. Ruby slaps his hand away. "Suck it out." Robin moves his mouth to Ruby's ass. He tastes the fifty, puts his teeth on it and pulls it out. His tongue goes right into Ruby's asshole and Ruby nearly faints with pleasure. Robin sucks and licks while Ruby bounces around on his face for a long time. Then Robin hears Ruby begin to gasp, gain his breath and gasp again and then he feels warm cum squirting all over his face.

'What fun,' he thinks, licking up what he can reach with his tongue.

Ruby falls on top of him, breathing hard. He finds Robin's ear and begins to lick it, purring "Baby, baby, baby" into it. By the time their hearts have slowed down to a normal pace, they are both fast asleep.

🐾

16

A DAILY DOSE OF DISASTERS

It is two o'clock the next afternoon by the time Robin gets home. His body aches from sleeping on Ruby's kitchen floor all night and his mind is a puddle from so much sex. He and Ruby did it again in the morning, in a more conventional manner, and then took a shower together and did it again. After that much sex his mind stops functioning.

As he enters the kitchen he notices a note from Charlie. "If you are not dead, call me at work. If you are, then forget it." 'That does not sound friendly,' he thinks. He searches for a soothing, innocent voice as he dials.

"Hi, honey. I'm home."

"You didn't even call. Anything could have happened to you. I was awake imagining all sorts of horrible things. Where were you anyway?" The anger and relief put Charlie near tears.

"I was with Ruby. He had to show off all his new loot and then it was late and I was too stoned to come home," he explains, leaving out a few details.

"Ah, the job was pulled off, was it? How much did they get?"

"Enough. Let's not talk about it on the phone. Look, I'm sorry. I just wasn't thinking. You forgive me?"

"Maybe. If you take me out to dinner."

"I'd love to, hon. But you forget I never see you. When *Too Much Heat in the Amazon* closes I'll take you out."

"Oh, goody goody." Charlie is smiling, bouncing up and down at his desk. "Oh, I'm glad you're O.K."

"You sound so sincere it could break my heart."

"Break it, baby," Charlie says, attempting his vamp voice, "I have to get off the phone. Mr. Monster thinks I should work

157

for my money. Can you imagine such a backward attitude in this advanced day and age?" They kiss their phones and hang up.

The cats begin to scream. "O.K., O.K." Robin hauls himself out of the sofa and walks to the kitchen. He hears a crunch and looks down. He has just stepped on a dead mouse. "Ah, my great hunters do it again." The mouse is a tiny baby. "So brave." Auden is purring and rubbing against Robin's leg. He picks the mouse up by its tiny tail and throws it in the garbage. The buzzer rings. "Oh, please, no. My nerves," he mumbles as he buzzes whoever it is in.

Before Robin can even think about collecting himself the door flies open and Rosa throws himself into the apartment. "How's my baby boy today?" he inquires.

"Juiceless. Milked to death."

"Sex is the only thing where too much is not enough. Remember when we were lovers? We were insatiable animals, clawing at each other all the time. It was heaven."

"That was ten years ago. I'm older now."

"Tireder, one might say."

"Speaking of tired, dear, where did you get that outfit?" Rosa is sporting Levi's, a flannel shirt and a leather jacket.

"It's clone drag."

"That I got right away."

"I can't help it. I'm in lust."

"Get real, Rosa. Is it the one you met in the bar last night?"

"The same. He is so sweet." Sweet takes him at least fifteen seconds to say. "He is mush on the inside but so butch on the outside."

"Sounds like a grilled cheese sandwich to me."

"He wants to take me away from all of this."

"Where is he planning to take you?"

"To Chelsea. He has a gorgeous duplex there, a little small, but very expensive. And from Chelsea to the circuit. You know, all the chic gay watering holes." Robin looks skeptical. "I've never been on the circuit. It might be grand."

"Rosa, what has happened to you? You gave up clones just last week and you hate the circuit."

"I'm overcome by lust. I'll recover, I'm sure, but I'm in such a state. My heart says no, no, but my groin says yes, yes. I hate being in lust."

"Being in love is better?" Robin asks.

"At least when you're in love you can fantasize about a life together, but lust, dear, all I think about is the bed."

"And you can't live on your back."

"Ah, but we try, don't we?" Rosa pats Robin's cheek and gives him a sweet smile.

"Have you heard anything today about the accident?" Robin asks, recovering from Rosa's breathless onslaught, returning to what he quaintly thinks of as the real world.

"That ghastly thing. I heard it's still emitting radioactivity and that some clowns called Met Ed, who apparently own this contraption, say it's nothing."

"They probably don't live near it."

"I assume they have all left for Paris. Maybe that's what I should do with my new wealth. Scarlet is going to California tomorrow."

"For the earthquake season?"

"For the sake of the fetus and the future." Rosa leaps up from the sofa. "I must dash. I have to pick up my money from Ruby, zoom home, shower and try to pull myself back to beauty and then dash back to Jeff's. Yes, that's his name, clones do have names you know, for more stoke and poke."

"Stoke and poke?"

"Get it hot and stick it in. I tell you this lust stuff has turned my life into a pornographic movie. I just want him to finger my fuck hole all day long."

"Except nobody ever gets depressed in porn movies."

"I can see why. They are so busy keeping it up with bites and licks and sucks..."

"Rosa, stop, you'll get me hot."

"I used to be able to get you hot, so hot you'd beg for it."

"I barely remember."

"You would repress the best thing that ever happened to you. That's it for now. I'm too hot to be stopped."

"You will have to pick up your money," Robin chuckles. "We threw it all over the apartment and then fucked on it."

"Is it soggy with cum?" Rosa asks as if he is speaking about dog shit.

"Only the fifties."

"That's something. I'll see you during my next break from the hot meat man," and he flies out the door.

'Rosa and a clone. I can't believe it. You can't count on anything anymore,' Robin broods. The cats wander into the room yelling for food. Robin gets up, opens a can for each. "Eat yourselves into oblivion." He sits back on the sofa and stares at the wall.

A half hour later he is still staring at the wall. His mind is not working. Slowly he notices that anxiety is creeping into him. Then apprehension. He feels threatened and scared. 'It's that fucking accident,' he thinks. 'I should not be alone during these bad times.' As he stares at the wall for another half hour the feelings become more definite and more intense. The thought of going to visit someone comes to him. When he stands up he is dizzy. He holds on to the arm of the couch to steady himself. He takes two steps and stops. He is not going to make it. He retreats to the sofa and the comfort of the blank wall.

The phone rings. He picks up the receiver and grunts.

"I presume I'm speaking to a gorilla." It is Emma.

He grunts again.

"I suppose you know by now that it is still leaking that goddamn stuff and the wind is blowing in our direction."

"Should we leave town?"

"Scarlet is going to San Francisco."

"I know. How long do we have to get out?"

"They're not saying shit. Everything is under control, they say. Those lying fuckers. What do they care if we all die hideously painful deaths."

"Whatever happens, they'll make money off it."

"I did get laid."

"Oh, me too. Maybe disasters bring out the libido in everyone. Who with?"

"Scarlet."

"A mother to be?"

"We decided to celebrate new life. With death rays pouring in on us, somebody has to. Besides, I thought it might be different with her being pregnant and all."

"Was it?"

"Not that I could tell. Fuck, there's my buzzer." She drops the receiver on the floor and kicks the phone over as she runs for the buzzer. Robin's ear hurts. She recovers the phone. "Sorry. Can't imagine who that... Maybellene!" Emma screams into the phone.

"She shot a building," Robin hears Maybellene yelling over and over in the background. "She shot a building. She shot a building." Emma drops the receiver again and goes to hold Maybellene. "She shot a building. The police have her. Come with me."

"Who? What building?"

"Flow. She shot the J. P. Stevens building. She flipped out on something." Robin can hear Maybellene screaming and crying.

He yells "Hello" into the phone.

Emma hears him. "Sit down and get a hold on yourself. Robin's on the phone." She puts Maybellene into a chair and looks for the receiver. She kicks it, then picks it up.

"What's going on there?" Robin yells.

"I don't know. Calm down."

"Do you need help. Money or something?"

"Maybellene, do we need money?"

"They're not going to let her out. Ever. She shot a building."

"But you can't kill a building. Now calm down. Robin, if I

161

need you I'll call. Meet us in the bar later. Keep in touch."

"Sure." Robin hangs up the phone, completely unhinged, and calls for Auden and Gloria. He hears nothing. He needs them. He lurches out of the living room down the long hall into the bedroom. They are passed out on the bed, curled around each other. Gloria raises his white, furry head, blinks at Robin twice and falls back asleep. "How can you sleep at a time like this?" They do not move. "The world may be ending and you're drugged out on food." He grabs his Mexican sweater off a nail and goes out the door.

The hall lights are out. It is kohl black. Robin can see nothing. He feels for the rail and lets his hand lead him down the dark stairway. At the bottom some light comes through the door window. He lets go of the railing and opens the door.

There is a short hall to the street where the mailboxes are. He opens his mailbox and takes out a letter from a lawyer who is suing him over an old doctor's bill, a pamphlet from the overpriced supermarket telling him what their bargains are this week and a letter from an insurance company refusing to give him theft insurance. He thrusts all of this into his pocket and looks up at the open door to the street. A tall man on roller skates suddenly appears in the doorway, jumps up the small step and skates towards him. Robin freezes. He does not know this man. He stops in front of Robin and pulls out a gun.

"Your money and your drugs. Now." Robin's mind floods with fear. His vision blurs. He can see light behind the man. The street is only a few feet away. The man rolls closer. He looks like a killer to Robin. "Now," he hisses at Robin.

Robin's mouth starts to move. In a few seconds sounds begin to come out "... Rockefeller, why not rob him? He's got the money, not me..."

"Your money and your drugs or I'll blow you away."

"You're right on the street." Robin points to Second Avenue.

"I got wheels. I can move. Stop this shit." Robin looks at the gun. 'Is it real?' His vision is foggy from fear. 'I'll pretend it is.' He reaches into his pocket and takes out his money—thirteen dollars and change—and hands it over. The man takes it.

"Drugs. Give me your drugs."

"I don't have any."

"Everybody's got drugs, baby. Hand them over." Robin notices the man is young, early twenties, cute, blond and his hand is shaking. "You're making me very nervous. I might lose control." Robin pulls a Quaalude out of his shirt pocket and hands it to the man. The man takes it.

"This is a drag. I was just robbed yesterday," Robin whines.

The man rolls backwards. 'Maybe he'll fall on the step. Fall on the step, fall on the step.' Robin's mind takes up a quick mantra. The man jumps backwards off the step and is gone. Robin falls against the mailboxes with relief. 'It's only money. I am not hurt. It doesn't matter. It is only money.' Repeating this litany learned from too many robberies, he composes himself. He walks out onto the street and hurries to the bar.

It is nearly crowded; the mood is nearly happy. Robin walks up to Bruce, slumped gloomily against the bar.

"Can you buy me a drink? Someone on roller skates just mugged me." Bruce looks at him with glazed-over eyes. Robin is not sure he recognizes him. "Are you all right?"

"Barnaby told me it was over. Just like that. Over. Nothing. Dead. Death."

"Maybe his injuries have changed him."

"And what am I supposed to do?"

"Stop loving him."

"Over. Dead." He speaks in a monotone with a slight slur.

"I'd give you a Quaalude but the bandit on roller skates took my last one."

"I've had two already. But I can still feel. Fuck it."

"Buy me a drink."

"Sure." Robin orders a double scotch and drinks half of it in one gulp.

"Love is shit."

"Sometimes."

"I'll give it up."

"What will you do instead?"

"I'll take up a craft. I'll crochet again." The slur in his voice is more noticeable. He weaves back and forth. His hands are trembling. Robin looks around and spots Rosa and his clone chatting near the pool table. Rosa spots him and points to his friend and fans his face frantically with his left hand. 'Rosa is giving too much give as usual,' Robin thinks, turning back to Bruce, whose eyes are closed and whose body is nearly limp. 'I must remember to be amused by all of this, otherwise I might as well go live in Peoria,' he thinks, trying to revive Bruce.

"Come on, hon. Wake up and go home. You'll feel better tomorrow."

"Maybe there won't be a tomorrow."

"Well, then you'll definitely feel better, won't you?"

Suddenly Maybellene and Emma are at his side. He jumps with surprise.

"It's too gross. They've got her locked up. We couldn't even see her. I need about ten drinks." Maybellene slaps money on the bar.

"Did you find out what happened?"

"Yeah. Get this. Flow walks into J. P. Stevens corporate headquarters in midtown someplace, goes to the elevators, takes out a gun and starts shooting the numbers out above the elevator doors. Can you imagine? Everyone scattered. She is screaming, 'This one is for brown lung disease; this one is for union busting; this one is for racism; this is for Norma Rae,' until the gun is empty. Then she walks out the front door. The cops got her on the street in front. They think she is crazy."

"So she is. Let's drink to her." Robin raises his glass. "To crazy runamuck revolutionary dykes." They smile at each other wistfully.

"The cops said they'll probably send her to a nut house."

"Give her lots of Thorazine and shock treatments until she

is normal again." Emma can feel rage welling up inside. "She didn't hurt a soul."

"That's why they think she's crazy," Maybellene asserts. "If she'd killed a couple of people, that they could understand. I'm just afraid they'll torture her for names or something. Oh, I'll never see her crazed insanity again," and Maybellene begins to cry. Emma puts her arms around her as Bruce slumps to the floor. The three quickly surround him and pull him to his feet. His eyes open slightly.

"Give me a glass of water." When the bartender hands it to him, Robin throws it in Bruce's face. Everyone screams and Bruce opens his eyes wide. Rosa and his friend rush across the room to see what dish is going down.

"What's all the screaming? Tell. Tell."

"Bruce is gone on ludes. Why don't you help him home? He lives right near you." Rosa looks slightly annoyed. Robin is persistent. "Your friend can help. Butch must be good for something."

Rosa pokes Robin in the stomach, but his friend smiles and says, "Sure. Let's go." They lift Bruce up and walk him out the door.

"It's because of Barnaby?" Emma is concerned.

"Yeah. Barnaby said kaputnick, later for you, kid."

"Thank the goddess I don't have to put up with men anymore. One is slimier than the next. How can you go on being a fag?" Maybellene acts incredulous.

"A man-hating fag. Oh, please. Let's not dwell on life's tragic ironies. I am trying to keep my spirits up." A joint moves into his hand and he draws very deeply on it, just in case it doesn't pass his way again. He looks at the door and his spirits are up. "Two reasons I'm still a fag just walked in the door," he whispers deliciously to Maybellene.

Charlie and Ruby see them at once. Ruby puts his hand on Charlie's neck and steers him to the group at the bar. Everyone kisses everyone else, very friendly and smoochy. Robin spurts out his roller skate saga and Maybellene tells the shoot-up at

J.P. Stevens story and Emma gives the collapsing rejected lover dish.

"And it's still giving off radioactivity," Ruby offers in the spirit of continual bad news. "The radio says they may order an evacuation 'cause it may melt down."

"Should we leave?" Emma asks the group. No one answers.

Finally Charlie, bothered by the silence, says, "Where would we go?" Everyone looks blank. Charlie looks at Robin intensely and continues. "Can we take the cats?"

Robin reaches out and glazes Charlie's hand. "I think we should die where we live." Everyone comes to life.

"Let's not get hysterical," Emma says hysterically.

Robin modifies his terms. "I'd rather get poisoned where I live than in some cheap motel on some crumbling highway in some strange, hostile place."

Ruby starts to chant, "You can't see it; you can't hear it; you can't taste it; you can't smell it; you can't feel it. It can penetrate your flesh and you will not know it for thirty years until your body goes berserk and pain overcomes you. It is invisible and lethal."

"Invisible and lethal," Maybellene snorts. "The perfect weapon against us. We don't even know they're getting us. We just get stoned and lay around and then one day we die horrid deaths."

Robin sneers, "When we can't work anymore we're dead. How convenient for them."

Charlie, still concerned about the cats, asks, "Are we going to stay here through it?"

"Sure. We'll have an end-of-the-world party."

"Here at the Terminal Bar?"

"It will be the first annual end-of-the-world party." Everyone is so delighted that they each order another drink and prepare a boisterous toast to spending the end of the world together.

17

QUEERS DISHING THE END OF THE WORLD

"It's getting worse," Maybellene says ominously over the phone.

"Which one is getting worse?" Robin quickly goes over a list of crises in his mind.

"They fear a meltdown. Turn on WBAI and scare yourself to death."

"I'm already scared."

"Pregnant women and children are being evacuated. And the wind is blowing in our direction."

"And what are you going to wear for the end of the world?" Robin asks with as much sarcasm as he can manage.

"I thought black leather and rhinestones might work."

"I'm doing red and black. Revolutionary to the end. Does everyone know about the party?"

"I think so. Oh, it's so hard not to let the end of the world get you down."

"Keep busy."

"I am. I'm off to the police station to see about Flow. Maybe they'll let us talk to her. Scarlet has a lawyer working on it, which I guess means we'll have to organize a defense fund. You know how lawyers love to charge money. Bye."

She had called while Robin was masturbating. He goes back to the bedroom and lies down. His cock is limp. "Once more, for old time's sake," he says to it and with a little coaxing it gets hard. He tries to conjure up an orgy in the woods but his imagination fixates on a big mushroom cloud and his cock goes limp. 'The end of the world isn't very sexy,' he thinks and gets up and dresses.

He waters the plants, explaining to them that they may

either die soon or mutate madly. He feeds the cats, even though they aren't asking for food, telling them it may be their last supper. They ignore him and inhale their food. He walks into the living room, turns the radio on to WBAI and sits on the lavender sofa.

"What is happening is that a hydrogen bubble is forming in the top of the core of the reactor. It is getting larger. If it continues to expand it will force the water out of the core. As the water is forced out, at some point, the top of the fuel rods will be exposed. They will quickly overheat, since it is the water which keeps them cool, and when they become hot enough, they will melt. This will release an enormous amount of radioactivity into the atmosphere."

Suddenly, Robin can no longer be alone. He calls Charlie at work.

"Are you listening to BAI?"

"Yeah. Are you?"

"Yeah. I can't be alone right now. I'm going to the bar."

"I should be there with you."

"You're damn right. What a day to have to go to work."

"Mr. Monster doesn't care if it's Armageddon."

"Does he even know?"

"I told him and he said the media was hysterical. Can you imagine? Maybe it will at least make him sterile so he can't breed any more little monsters."

"This must be very heavy for the hets. Their very reason for feeling superior to us is on the line. They might all become sterile."

"Oh, here he comes. I'll come to the bar when I finish. Love ya."

"Boys, where are my boys?" Robin yells. Auden immediately walks into the living room yelling. Gloria zooms from the other end of the apartment and leaps onto the back of the sofa. Robin opens the glass jar filled with catnip that sits on the round table and sprinkles some around. The cats sniff cautiously, then quickly lick it up. They roll around on the floor, Auden opening his mouth wide and screaming, Gloria purring like an old Mixmaster. "There. I thought you should be stoned when people finally and completely fuck it up for you." He sprinkles more on the floor and all over them as they roll with delight. The phone rings.

"I've got some hot news for you." Ruby sounds conspiratorial. Robin knows that is not a good sign.

"Oh, I'm not ready, I'm sure, whatever it is."

"I just met a man who works as a busboy at a private club that Henry Kissinger goes to for lunch once in a while. This guy says that Kissinger has always got a lot of protection around him, secret service men or bodyguards. And, get this, somebody else always tastes the wine first."

"Sounds like a scared man to me."

"Certainly cautious. And probably ready for the likes of you, sweetheart. I don't think you are going to be able to kidnap him."

"Shit. I'll have to get a new fantasy together. Do you have any you could lend me?"

"I want to fuck in a big tub filled with fresh filet of sole."

"You are impossibly straight. No faggot would ever fantasize about fucking a filet of sole."

"Yeah? Well, give me a faggot fantasy."

Robin thinks for a second. "You see a slim young Puerto Rican boy in the bar. He is leaving, but at the door he hesitates. He turns his head and smiles at you. You follow him out the door and down the street until you both find yourself looking in the same window at some old junk. He turns to you . . . I think I'll save that one for tomorrow, it might be a slow day. Now I need something that's political and action-packed. The first gay, progressive senator."

"Sounds boring. Look who you'd have to hang out with. All those other senators." Robin begins to think seriously about his fantasy deprivation.

Ruby interrupts his musings. "What about becoming the first out, progressive movie star, making scads of money and preserving your integrity?"

"That's a fantasy for sure," Robin snorts and moves on. "I fall in love with a multimillionaire, not knowing he is a millionaire, of course; otherwise I'd never fall in love with him. Then he says to me that he has fifty million that he wants me to give away for him to help make a revolution. That has real possibilities."

"What about a gun runner for Latin American leftists? You could do it it all in drag. They'd never connect a drag queen up with a gun operation. Or we could do it as a group of drag queens. We'd pretend we were off on a vacation and drive through Mexico with the guns."

"I've noticed how eager Mexico is to have the drag queens of America come down there to party. Maybe I'll develop the general strike fantasy. It does seem to be getting stronger these days. But there is a problem. I can imagine how everyone could get pissed off enough at the same time to all go out on strike at once. Then there is all this energy and creativity and we start to make a new world. But then I always see some slimy, crooked fascist men taking over the whole thing and we're right back to now. I have to work on it." Robin pauses and realizes that he feels better. "So nice of you to call. I'm much cheered up."

"Maybe you should figure out what's going to happen when the radioactive cloud blows our way."

"You mean an end-of-the-world fantasy?"

"Yeah. That seems more practical."

"I'm not interested. They always turn out to be so grotesque." Robin sighs. "I expect you to be a bundle of laughs at the party tonight."

"I'm writing a new song, 'Mutation Blues,' for the occasion. See you there." They kiss their phones desperately.

From the radio he hears an interview with an old couple who live near the possible meltdown.

The man says, "We are terrified and have no place to go."

The woman says, "We have always lived here and now this."

The reporter sounds near tears when she says, "Thank you for talking to us.'

Robin walks into the closet and finds a large piece of cardboard. The cats run into the closet and refuse to come out. "That's disgraceful. You can't be in a closet on a day like today." They both pretend he does not exist. He finds some Magic Markers and makes a sign of pink and lavender with trees and flowers. It says, "Welcome to the End."

The lights are on in the hallway as he goes cautiously down the stairs with the sign under his arm. When he gets to the street, he turns right and sees the limousines. 'Their fallout shelters must be down here,' he thinks. There are two of them. Only one has a driver in it. The other one is empty. 'If only I was prepared to do something. What have I got? A sign. And I'm alone. Never act alone. Flow was wrong. Couldn't she have found at least one other person who shared her fantasy? Stay calm. It's a missed opportunity. There are lots of those. But it is getting too late for missed opportunities. I should have planned for this. I should have known that at some point I'd find one unattended and been prepared to act.' His mind is tumbling around like a clothes drier. His feet walk him directly to the bar. Someone has sprayed "Repent Queers Before It Is Too Late" on the plywood window. Someone has answered "It Already Is."

The bar is nearly empty. 'It's early, I guess.' He easily finds a stool and sits on it. He lays the sign on the bar with the words showing. The bartender reads it. "It's because of Three Mile Island. It may go at any moment. So we thought we'd have a party," Robin explains, trying to say it all at once so the bartender won't refuse.

He laughs. "It won't be that great for business, but then business isn't that great anyway." He takes the sign and tapes it on the mirror behind the liquor bottles. Robin is pleased.

"What are you, the decorating committee?" Robin is startled by Barnaby's voice. He turns on his stool and sees him smiling, weaving, standing very near to him. He holds out his arms and welcomes Barnaby back into his life.

"I love seeing you. I heard you weren't receiving callers so I didn't call. How are you?" Barnaby steps back a little to show him a black and swollen ear. He raises his hair, revealing a wound on his forehead still held together with stitches. His eyelid, a reddish color, blinks.

"I get dizzy easily. I can hardly drink at all. I'm tired a lot."

"What happened?"

"I don't remember anything. When I came to I was in the hospital. When they brought me in I looked so much like a bum, reeking of alcohol and bleeding all over the place, that they barely treated me at all. They didn't even take any X rays of my head. They sewed me up and told me to leave. They figured they weren't going to make any money off me so they wanted me out fast. I couldn't stand up. They still told me to leave. I yelled at them. Then Maybellene arrived and took me home in a cab. They were throwing me back onto the street. I couldn't stand up or function at all. If I'd lived on the street I would have been dead in a day."

"I guess we have to give up being numb," Robin says. "We have to be ready for danger, prepared to act. I saw the limousines again tonight. One of them was empty. But I was alone and unprepared."

"I saw them too. Probably here to place bets with the bookies on the exact time of the meltdown." Barnaby's eyes close. He leans towards Robin until he is resting against him.

"I was angry sometimes at you for getting hurt so badly."

"Like blaming the Jews for the extermination camps," Barnaby says with sarcasm and a flicker of bitterness.

"A little. I couldn't figure out why. It seemed to unkind. I was embarrassed by it. Then I realized why. You blew it for the rest of us. The party's over. Our long debauch has to end. We can't stumble around unconscious and unprotected anymore. We've got to be awake."

Barnaby raises himself and looks at Robin. It is the saddest look Robin has ever seen. He speaks softly. "I can hardly bear to see any more of it. I don't want to see any more of it. I know too much."

"But you already know the worst. The rest will just be more details." Robin puts his arms around Barnaby and rubs his spine. Barnaby moans softly and Robin can feel him relax a little.

Barnaby pulls unsteadily away. His body quivers twice. He stands six feet up, sets his head in the right place and puts his hands to his sides to steady them. He is now prepared to get through to the end, as long as it doesn't take too long.

Robin turns away from the blackened ear and the scar and the red eye, feeling too vulnerable and too sad. 'The state won't even need to come and take us away. The thugs will have already gotten us,' he thinks bitterly.

"Now there's something to see." Barnaby tries to laugh and points to the door. Rosa is just entering. His face is nearly covered by a huge pair of round dark glasses. He wears a long blue cloth coat with a brown fur collar turned up to cover what little of his face is not hidden by the glasses. He has a cap pulled down over his head. He walks cautiously up to them.

He kisses Barnaby and makes a fuss over his injuries. "Scars are very sexy. Get some hot story together about how you got them and the fags will drool."

"What is this outfit?" Robin inquires.

"I can't stay for the party. I have to get out of town until this thing cools down. Jeff is going to take me into hiding."

"Rosa, what is going on?" Robin is impatient and worried.

"I'm friends with this Mexican cook at the restaurant and I knew one of his kids was real sick and they pay him shit, you know, 'cause he's illegal. After our little," he lowers his voice, "you know what, I called him and said I wanted to give him some money for the kid. He was really happy. I think he knew where the money came from, but he was cool. Anyway today he calls me up and says he overheard two of the bosses talking about me and the you know what. Just talk. They've got no proof."

"You sure about that?"

"Yeah. We wore gloves and everything. But I got scared and thought I'd leave town for a little."

"Where's your hideout?"

"Jeff's friend has a place in one of the Hamptons. So he's taking me there."

"My, my," Robin exclaims. "What a fancy crook."

"If I have to hide in terror it might as well be in the Hamptons," Rosa says in his grandest diva tone.

Robin turns to order a new drink and notices his sign. "Any news from the meltdown?"

"I heard that the bubble is stabilizing, whatever that means. ABC acted like it was good news," Rosa answers.

"You believe them?" Barnaby asks sarcastically.

"I barely believe myself anymore, let alone anything ABC might be saying."

Robin notices that three other fags at the bar have seen the sign and are asking the bartender about it. They turn and smile at him and raise their glasses in a toast. He smiles back and toasts.

Ruby throws open the door, steps in and belts out, "O Lord, please don't let it meltdown all over me."

Someone yells, "One more time."

He falls to his knees, raises his hands and wails, "Please, oh please, don't let it meltdown all over me." He jumps up and winks at the scattered applause.

"What are you on?" Robin demands.

"I'm high on life."

"Maybe not for long."

"What did you take?" Robin will not be denied.

"A little Q, a little grass and a couple of drinks..."

"That's what you call life?" Robin is triumphant.

"Oh, babe. How's by you?" Ruby hugs Barnaby. "Let me see. Oh, nasty."

"Ruby, I'm going into hiding for a while." As Rosa is telling Ruby about the small alarm, Bruce comes into the bar.

174

When he sees Barnaby he thinks, 'I should leave.' But he wants to see him for a bit, be in the same room with him for a while. He says a quiet hello to his friends, one filled with the dignity of the occasion, orders a scotch and retires to the corner of the bar.

"Do you want to flee town with us? We could have a real den of thieves."

"You forget, dear Rosa, they don't know me. I never worked there." Ruby is pleased with his cunning. He lights two joints and passes them in opposite directions.

"Maybe Bruce wants to flee with us."

"Here, take him a joint." Rosa flounces across the room to sit with Bruce.

Maybellene and Emma arrive. Maybellene is beside herself. Emma is trying to be strong.

"They have her in Bellevue for observation. We couldn't see her."

"If you aren't nuts when you go in there, you will be by the time you get out," Barnaby offers.

"Oh, hon. You came out. How are you feeling?"

"Terminal."

"For once you are in the right place at the right time."

Emma notices Robin's sign. "I guess it hasn't happened yet."

"We're all still here."

"Is Scarlet here?" Emma asks anxiously.

"No, I thought she went off to California."

"She changed her mind. I hope she comes. She's a mess."

"How can she have a baby at a time like this?" Barnaby demands of Emma.

"That's why she is a mess. All her resolve seems to be melting away."

Charlie saunters in and strolls to Robin's side. They kiss. "I was fired," Charlie says with a grin on his face.

"Fired! For what?"

"I told Mr. Monster that I thought he was stupid, indifferent to the suffering around him and a petty and

175

tyrannical boss.''

"I can see why he might have fired you. So what now?''

"If it's over, I hardly need a job and if it isn't, I'll find another one.'' Charlie feels wise and on top of it. It shows in his face. Robin puts his arm around his waist and lays his head on his shoulder.

"How are we gonna know when it happens?'' Charlie asks the group. They are standing in a circle, touching each other in small ways for some small comfort.

"I guess we'll have to wait for the morning papers.''

The door opens and Scarlet walks in. She stops. They turn to greet her, but the look of disbelief on her face stops them. She puts her left hand into her pants and then pulls it out. Her fingers are red. "Blood,'' she says quietly. She puts her right hand into her pants and then pulls it out. Those fingers are red also. "Blood.'' She approaches the circle, holding both hands out in front of her. The red fingers shake slightly. She walks up to each person and shows them the blood. Her heart fills with sadness and she begins to cry. They slip her into the center of the circle. They stroke her and pat her and rub her. Finally Emma takes her in her arms and whispers, "It's better this way.''

"I wanted it to be all right.''

"We all did.'' Emma releases her. "Do you have a tampon?''

"Yeah.'' The circle breaks for Scarlet. She walks slowly to the toilet.

"It's too grim,'' Rosa says, staring off into space.

"It is an end-of-the-world party,'' Barnaby answers.

"I hope next year's will be a little more upbeat.''

"I wouldn't count on it.''

Larry Mitchell was born July 12, 1938 in Muncie, Indiana. By 1960 he was safely in New York City. He now lives on the Lower East Side of Manhattan with a boy friend and a cat. He last appeared on the New York stage with the Pink Satin Bombers' Evening of Faggot Theatre. He teaches Sociology and Women's Studies at the City University of New York on Staten Island for fun and money and runs Calamus Press out of his apartment for fun. He flees in the summers to Lavender Hill, a gay settlement outside of Ithaca, New York.

Books by Larry Mitchell

1982   *The Terminal Bar: A Novel*

1977   *The Faggots and Their Friends Between Revolutions*

1972   *Great Gay in the Morning* (with The Lavender Hill Group)

1970   *Willard Waller on The Family, Education, and War* (with William J. Goode and Frank Furstenberg, Jr.)

OTHER BOOKS FROM CALAMUS

FALSE CLUES $3.50
Poems by Ron Schreiber

FLOWERS $4.00
Poems by Richard Ronan
Drawings by Bill Rancitelli

THE FAGGOTS AND THEIR FRIENDS
BETWEEN REVOLUTIONS $5.00
Text by Larry Mitchell
Drawings by Ned Asta

MERCY DROP AND OTHER PLAYS $5.00
by Robert Patrick

QUEER FREE $5.00
by Alabama Birdstone

THE TERMINAL BAR: A NOVEL $6.00
by Larry Mitchell

DON THE BURP AND OTHER STORIES $5.00
by Ray Dobbins

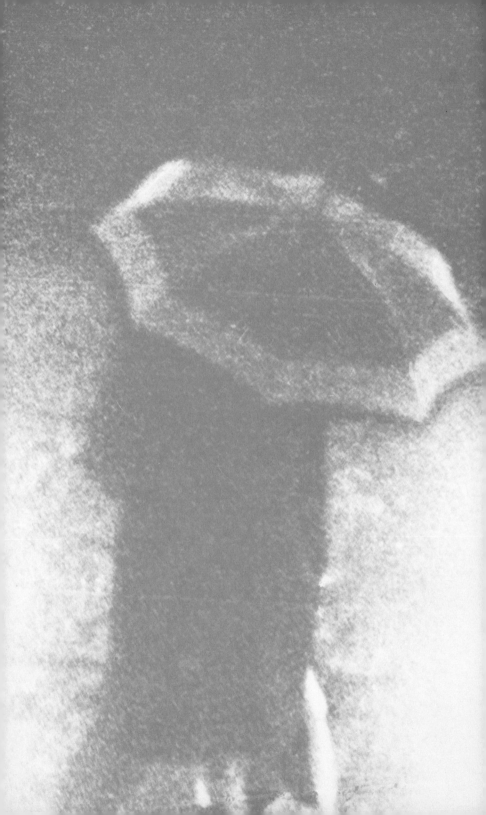